THE PUPPET MASTER

MORGAN HUNTER

authorHOUSE®

AuthorHouse™
1663 Liberty Drive
Bloomington, IN 47403
www.authorhouse.com
Phone: 1 (800) 839-8640

Published by AuthorHouse 03/06/2019

ISBN: 978-1-7283-0335-2 (sc)
ISBN: 978-1-7283-0334-5 (e)

Print information available on the last page.

This book is printed on acid-free paper.

THE PUPPET MASTER

The Puppet Master-Men who marry to manipulate their wives as servants. Non people to do their every bidding. The great manipulator who has people doing his every deeds. A person who convinces you that his only desire is your happiness. When in fact his only desire is his own happiness, at the cost of all others. But Puppet Masters aren't all that easy to pick out of a crowd. They usually appear charming and fun to be with. That is until you say the magic words "I Do". Then they turn into someone you barely recognize.

At first you blame yourself. Have I put on a few too many pounds? Am I no longer pretty enough? Could I have kept the house even cleaner? Never realizing that none of these things would have made a difference, because it was never you he wanted. All he wanted was the part of you he could manipulate, control and yes sometimes terrorize. But it will take years into the marriage before you realize who you really married. And the thought will be chilling.

My Aunts use to talk about this kind of man who marries. They use to call it MarriageMare (Marriage/Nightmare). But I had always thought they were saying MerryMere. I really didn't know what it was, but it sounded scary just by the way they would discuss it in hushed whispers. Their eyes darting from side to side as though they were afraid they might be overheard. I was never quite sure what they were talking about, but I was sure I didn't want any part of it. If only I had been that lucky. But as you will see, life doesn't always turn out the way we expect it to. Welcome to MarriageMare at the hands of the Puppet Master.......

CHAPTER 1

Savannah looked around and smiled at all she had accomplished. It had been one endless struggle for her since the day she had been born. But she had succeeded despite the odds. Her children had all graduated from college now and had families of their own. She had finally moved into her dream home and succeeded at a career no one thought was possible.

There was a time in her life when she wondered if she'd ever make it. Her life had been one roller coaster ride after another. But she had always had an inner strength and courage few people possess. She had many people along the way who had tried to dampen her spirit, but she had succeeded despite them. She had chosen to keep her dreams and ideas to herself. Sharing them with no one. People seemed afraid of those who dared to dream of something better. But she had been to the depths of despair and hadn't liked what she had seen. She knew then that she needed to strive for something different. She knew this was a life she could never life with. She had to fight for her dream, because the life she was living was to painful.

Her mind began to wander back to where she believed her courage to fight and survive had all begun. To a small farming community she had grown up in. Raised by a mother who had blamed her children for everything that had ever gone wrong in her life. This is where Savannah had first learned the skills of being a survivor. To rise above the circumstances and succeed at any cost.

Her mother had been an only child, raised in a very prominent family and had never wanted for anything. She had grown up to believe that God had created her for her own self satisfaction and the world owed her a lifetime of fulfillment. She believed life was there for the taking and she should have her every desire granted. Up until she had meet Savannah's father this had been the case. But Savannah's father had been the one man who wasn't interested in a self absorbed, spoiled brat, no matter how rich she was.

As is usually the case with most spoiled children, they always want what they can't have. Savannah's mother was no exception. She pursued Savannah's father relentlessly. Convincing herself that he was the only man she could ever love. The fact that he wasn't interested only intrigued her more. She'd had dozen of men before him that had simply adored her. But their obvious adoration of her had left her bored and uninterested. For the first time in her life she had met someone who wasn't taken with her good looks or in love with her family's money. It was a challenge she couldn't walk away from. She had decided this was what she wanted and she would stop at nothing until she got it.

She finally wore him down and he agreed to take her out as a favor to his family. Not knowing that she had her sights set on him, they had thought she was just a charming young lady from their Church who was trying to be friendly to the family. There was no way they would have expected it to be anything else. Though they were a devotedly religious family and very loving, they were also desperately poor. Defiantly not in her social class. In fact they were a little surprised and somewhat flattered that she would have even considered being seen with their son in public. Her family had more money than any family had a right to. Her family's money opened doors that their family could only dream about.

They had struggled a lifetime just to put food on the table and a roof over their heads. The children in the family had worked at odd jobs since they had been very young, just to help the family out. It wasn't that their mother wasn't a hard worker herself, but with her husband having been killed in a farming accident shortly after the youngest child was born, there were just too many mouths to feed and not enough money to go around. She was too proud to take charity and no man in his right mind would marry her with all the children she had. So she and her family did the best they could with what they had and prayed for God's mercy for the rest. She was just so thankful that someone like Savannah's mother had been able to look past their poverty and see the true heart of their family.

But her mother's parents were outraged. They didn't care how descent a family her father came from. He was still poor and not worthy of their daughter. She was their only child and they were going to marry her into a family as wealthy and prominent as they were. She'd had many offers of marriage into these prominent families, but had turned them all down. They had never insisted on her marrying against her will, but they were not about to let her throw her life away either. If she was not happy with the offers she'd had so far, she would just have to wait until the right man, from the right family, came along. And this poor country boy, from the wrong side of town was defiantly not it. They didn't care what kind of fuss she put up, this was one time they were putting their foot down. They would do whatever it took to make sure she never dated him again. But they had underestimated their daughter. She had never been told No in her life and she wasn't about to hear it now.

She appeared on the surface to be the obedient daughter, doing as her family wished. She continued to go out with the respectable men her family approved of, even becoming quit fond of one of them. But behind their backs she continued to see Savannah's father as well. Very innocently of course. She first won the hearts of the family by continuing to stop by on behalf of Church business. With a family their size, there was always someone sick or someone to invite to the many social activities the Church offered. It wasn't long before she was a regular visitor to their home. And it wasn't long before the family fell hopelessly in love with her. All but Savannah's father that is.

It wasn't that he disliked her actually. She seemed nice enough, though at times a little vain and shallow. But he expected that from someone as wealthy as she was. It was just that he wasn't ready to date anyone seriously. He had grown up in a large family, working hard and struggling every day just to have something to eat and a place to sleep. He knew how hard it was to be married and take care of a family and he wasn't about to tie himself to that ball and chain just yet. He planned on marrying someday and having a family, but for now he just wanted to enjoy life without all the responsibility. He knew he should have been thrilled that someone as pretty and rich as she was, was attracted to him. But the truth was he wasn't.

For the first time in his life he had a chance to think only about himself. Have a little fun and figure out what made him happy. It wasn't that he was self centered and absorbed with himself. It was just the first time he hadn't needed to figure out what was best for the family. His siblings were getting older now and starting families of their own. Reducing the number of children still at home to care for. This had lightened his load tremendously. His siblings still helped out, even with families of their own and the pressures of supporting the family had eased considerably. This was why he was in no hurry to start the whole process again with his own family. But he had no way of knowing he would be no match for the selfish whims of Savannah's mother.

In all fairness though, she was in quit a dilemma herself. She liked to have fun and play by her own rules. Never aware that her actions could really have consequences. After all she had never had to account for anything she had ever done in her life. But that luxury would soon come to an end. Her many adventures in the back seats of her boyfriends cars, including Savannah's father's, had left her pregnant and terrified. The social backlash and public scorning she would receive if she didn't do something fast was almost overwhelming.

She went to her boyfriend, from the prominent family, her family liked so well and that she was sure was the father of her child. Just the shear amount of times they had been intimate would have made him the likely father. Most of the other men she had slept with, including Savannah's father had been no more than once or twice. They were very unlikely to have fathered her child. Which all considered was probably for the best anyway. She really liked this guy and he seemed to be really fond of her too. She was sure they would make a very striking couple and neither family would have any objections to this very smart alliance of two powerful and wealthy families.

All in all she was pretty happy with the way things were working out. She was really attracted to Savannah's father too, but this was a good trade off and would make her family very happy. She couldn't say she was really sorry the way things had happened, other than her partying days would soon be coming to an end. But that too would not be forever. Only until she could have the baby and leave it with the live-in nanny. A minor inconvenience as she saw it. But she could never have anticipated the reaction her boyfriend would have.

He went into a complete rage. So icy and cruel was his response that she was momentarily stunned. She could not believe what he was saying. He informed her that he had no intentions of marrying her or anyone else right now and when he did it would not be to some cheap, dressed-up trash like her who slept around. (Never mind that he was as guilty as she was in that area). He was going on to law school after college and start a brilliant law career just like his father. If she thought any different she was crazy. If she dared tell anyone that he was the father he would crucify her. He would tell anyone that cared to listen that she was loose and would sleep with anyone. He was surprised she hadn't caught a good case of something yet, the amount of men she had been with.

She could not believe the cruelty of his words and

actions. He could not have struck her with force and caused anymore pain. She was so crushed and broken when she left, it was a miracle she had managed to make it home. She had never imagined what just happened, could have ever happened to her. She had seriously thought of ending her life at that moment but decided against it. After all he had done to her she wouldn't let him have this final victory too.

With her and the baby gone, all his problems would have been solved. Even though she was sure he meant every word he said and would never be a part of their lives. With her alive and carrying his child she could at least have the satisfaction of making him sweat a little. As long as she and the baby lived, he had no way of knowing whether she would one day throw caution to the wind and show-up on his door step anyway. Demanding he claim their child as his own. Small victory though it was, at the moment it was all she had to hold on to.

For a fleeting moment abortion had also come to mind. That would surely solve both their problems. But that was a risky business at best. In this day and age, only back alley abortionist were available. Even if she wasn't somewhat concerned that she would instantly go to Hell if she had the procedure done, there was the question of where to have one done. She had heard some of their servants talking about abortions one day in the kitchen as she was walking by. They might be able to help her find someone, but there was always the chance they might leak the information of her situation to her parents. After all, they were employed by her parents and their first loyalty would naturally be to them. It was a chance she couldn't take. If they found out she was pregnant with no hope of marriage, she might as well be dead.

She didn't know what to do or who to turn to for advice. She had never been in a situation before that her parents couldn't fix for her. She thought of Savannah's father, but it seemed unfair to dump this on him. However, in her current situation, she really didn't have the luxury of worrying about what was fair and what wasn't. It wasn't fair that she was pregnant and without a husband either. But that was the current situation. She decided that her only hope was Savannah's father. She would lay the situation out before him and see if he had any helpful advice for her.

As she began to tell Savannah's father about how she was pregnant and scared out of her mind. He gently reached over and took her hand. Laying his other hand on top of her's. Gently caressing it as he did. He smiled and told her not to worry about anything. He would do what was right by her. He knew being intimate with her those few times could result in this very situation. He was older and should not have let the situation go that far. He was not rich by any means, but he would do what ever it took to make sure she had a good life. He knew what it was like to care for a family and he reassured her everything would be just fine.

Savannah's mother almost laughed out loud. She was so relieved she could barely contain herself. What a perfect plan! She couldn't have dreamed up anything better. She knew she owed it to him, to tell the truth. But she was running out of options. If he thought he was the father, so be it. She wasn't about to tell him any differently and she knew the father of her child wouldn't either. He would be so relieved when he found out, he would probably weep for joy. She had a nagging feeling that what she was doing was really wrong. Maybe even evil. But she just ignored it. She didn't have time for guilt right now. She had bigger problems. He didn't seem too crushed over the idea of marrying her anyway and he certainly could have done worse. She might have tricked him into marriage, but he would have a much richer life thanks to her.

She knew her parents would be outraged when they told them. But she also knew they had no other option but to consent. It was unheard of for a daughter of her social standing to be pregnant and unmarried. Their entire family would be socially ostracized and she knew they couldn't stand that thought anymore than she could. They would do what needed to be done, no matter how bitter the situation was to swallow. They were society's elite and feelings rarely played in to the decisions they made. They would be furious with her for a while, but in the end would make the best of it.

She had little hope that Savannah's father would ever truly be accepted into the family, but for now this was all she had to work with. Conscience be damned! She was doing what needed to be done. If there had to be casualties along the way, it couldn't be helped. Her life was as important as his was and she would do anything she needed to, to survive. Including using anybody she could to help her. It may not be a pretty picture to look at, but it was life and she planned on making it as good for herself as she could.

To say that Savannah's mother's parents were outraged would have been an understatement. They were so enraged when Savannah's mother and father broke the news to them that they had ordered Savannah's father to leave their home at once and never return. They went on raging to Savannah's mother for what seemed like hours. Threatening

her with every conceivable punishment they could think of.
Savannah's mother had been wise enough to keep her mouth
shut and listen to the abuse. Realizing that in the end they
would come to the same conclusion she had. There was no
other choice for her but this one.

It had been a bitter pill for her parents to swallow. Their
only child, married to a man with no money and no future.
In their minds, this was as bad as it could be. They had,
had such hopeful dreams for her and she had thrown them
all away. Always taking what she wanted and thinking of
the consequences later. They knew deep down though, they
were as much to blame as she was. They had never denied her
anything and this was what had become of such leniency.
Now they would all pay for a lifetime of never setting limits.

CHAPTER 2

Savannah's grandparents finally relented and married their only child to Savannah's father. There was so much hostility in them that it could not be overlooked. But Savannah's father was determined to make the marriage work, whether his in-laws liked him or not. He would repay bitterness with kindness and hope they would eventually warm up to him. He hadn't planned on marrying this soon, but he certainly couldn't have asked for a better match. His marriage to Savannah's mother was more than he could have ever hoped for in a marriage.

His own family had felt the same way. His mother and siblings adored Savannah's mother and were happy that he had the good sense to grab her while he could. They spent every waking moment making her feel welcomed and loved by their family. They couldn't seem to do enough for her. Running errands, cleaning house, and cooking meals for her. Whatever they could think of to help her out. They realized early on in the marriage that she had no housekeeping skills and was clueless as to what it took to run a household. She was also sick most of the time due to the pregnancy and did little more than lie on the couch and throw-up. They had no idea how unhappy she really was.

Marriage was not at all what she thought it would be and she was already resenting how tied down and trapped she felt. There was never enough money for all the things she wanted and her husband had, to take a second job to provide any extras for her. She was constantly going to her family for money. Complaining that her husband was inept at taking care of her. She could never have imagined how hard being poor would be. To be honest they weren't exactly poor. But she had never lived anything but rich before and having to budget her money was not something she could get used to. She had never worried about paying bills or making money last before. She spent whatever she wanted and someone else had paid the bills. She had continued to do this in marriage as well, only now there wasn't enough money to cover what she spent. That forced her to constantly go to her parents for more.

But they were beginning to tire of her constant whining and complaining. They could see that Savannah's father was doing all he could to support the family and she should have realized being married to a working man would change her lifestyle. They had tried to tell her this many times before they had relented and agreed to let her marry him. But Savannah's mother was determined to live the lifestyle she had always lived. She was the only child her parents had and they owed it to her to help out. They certainly had enough money to give her without missing any of it. She didn't want to act grown-up and responsible. She had been spoiled and pampered her whole life and she liked it that way. She shouldn't have to give up the posh lifestyle she was accustom to, simply because she had married.

Once Savannah's sister was born, the situation got even

worse. Not only did Savannah's mother lack housekeeping skills, she also had no idea how to take care of a new born baby. Savannah's father would come home from work to find the baby screaming and hungry. Still in her pajama's and soaking wet from a diaper she had worn since the night before. Having been left in the crib all day long. Savannah's father was beside himself as to what to do. He couldn't work two jobs and take care of Savannah's sister as well. But he was concerned that the baby might not survive if someone didn't intervene. His only solution was to have one of his sisters take care of the baby, while his other sisters continued to take care of the house. He knew it was unfair to ask so much of his family, but he didn't have any other choice. Savannah's mother simply refused to be a part of any of it.

His family was great about it. They seemed happy to help in any way they could. In fact the sister who was in charge of taking care of Savannah's sister moved in with them so she could care for the baby full time. Savannah's father was grateful for her help. His sister was a natural at caring for the baby and seemed to be born with the skills of a mother. The baby was happy, clean and received his sister's undivided attention. This seemed to improve Savannah's mother's mood as well. This left her with the time she wanted to shop and visit with friends. Leaving the running of the house to her husband's family. Much like the way she had been raised. Only instead of hired servants, she had family members to help instead.

As unfair as this was to Savannah's father's family he knew there was nothing that could be done about it. They either helped or the baby would perish. He had gone to his wife's mother to ask that she help out as well, but she had refused. Stating that someone in her social position did not do common labor. She would be happy to visit the baby now and again, but under no circumstances would she help with the care of the baby. He was beginning to understand now why Savannah's mother was as worthless at housekeeping and motherhood as she was. She hadn't been taught the first thing about it. Maybe he could persuade his sisters to teach her the basics so she could lighten their burden a bit.

He must have been dreaming when he thought this plan would work. When he set down to explain to her how he had asked his sisters to help her learn the art of housekeeping she had went into a rage. Screaming that she too was not a common laborer who scrubbed floor, washed dishes and rinsed out dirty diapers. If that was the kind of women he wanted for a wife, he had picked the wrong one. She had far more important things she wanted to do with her life and she intended on doing them. But she was the one in for a surprise this time.

As she ate lunch and gossiped with her constant friend and companion she felt an all too familiar feeling come over her. The sight and taste of food was making her very ill. To the point where she felt she would throw-up any minute. The thought that she could possibly be pregnant again sent shock waves through her. Only an idiot would allow themselves to become pregnant again. Her mother had reminded her of this fact many times. It was the wife's duty to provide her husband with at least one heir, but that was all. After that, any smart wife would find a method for preventing future pregnancies at any cost. Her mother and her friends went to great lengths to share their knowledge in this department with one another. If Savannah's mother had paid a little closer attention when her mother and her friends were discussing this topic she might not be in this current situation.

After several weeks of doing nothing but throwing up, Savannah's mother could no longer deny that she was pregnant once again. The thoughts of that being possible left her almost suicidal. One pregnancy was a nightmare, two pregnancies was unthinkable. It took her weeks before she could force herself out of bed and to the doctor's office. Her worst fears were confirmed, or so she thought. But it would be several more months before she would learn she was actually carrying twins this time.

Savannah's father didn't know what to do. He was doing all he could now with just one child and they were barely getting by. With two more babies on the way he was sure they would sink. He couldn't ask his family to do anymore. They were already doing all they could. They had been helping since the birth of Savannah's sister and were still there. But this was more than any family member should be asked to do.

Savannah's mother's pregnancy went much like the first one had. She was sick all of the time and rarely able to leave her bed. The months went by like years until finally the delivery time arrived. She was simply glowing by the time she gave birth. Those in attendance thought it was the look of a proud mother, but it was really the look of a mother who was glad to be done with the whole mess. She would listen to her mother's advice on birth control this time. She now had three babies she didn't want and would not go through that experience again. It was unheard of in this day and age to refuse to have sex with your husband, so she would have to come up with another fail safe plan. As the birth control pill was still years away, that would not be a solution for her either.

She began spending hours with her mother and friends trying to get back to a normal life and pick up tips on preventing further pregnancies. She had even went to her own physician and begged him to do a surgical procedure to make her sterile, but he refused. In order to do this procedure he would have to have the signature of at least one other doctor and her husband's. Getting those two signatures was a hard sell, as most doctors at this time were male and could not understand a mother who did not want more children. They did offer her a ray of hope however, when they suggested that her husband have the surgery instead. It was a rather simple procedure for him and would require only their two signatures. After convincing her husband that another pregnancy would kill her, he relented and had the procedure done. But not in time to prevent a third pregnancy and a fourth child.

If her husband had not had the procedure done to ensure there would not be a fourth pregnancy she would have certainly ended her life. Her home and family life could only be described as a nightmare. With three babies under the age of three and a fourth one on the way she spent most of her time in bed. Partly because she was once again constantly sick, but mostly because she couldn't cope with the family situation. Because of this, the family was now being taken care of completely by Savannah's father's family and supported financially by Savannah's mother's family. Savannah's father was still working two full time jobs to support the family, but his income was no where near the amount of money needed to pay their bills.

It made him sick to realize he couldn't support his own family and needed to rely on his in-laws for help. Hopefully with his family size now completed he would be able to get back on his feet and no longer need their help. Four children would be a struggle to support on his income, but he would do all he could to make it possible. Hopefully after this birth, his wife would come around and spend more time with the children. Making it possible for his sisters to spend less time with them and begin lives of their own. Not that they were complaining, but they were young and deserved a life free from the drudgery they were now living.

At last the pregnancy came to an end and Savannah was born. The fourth child in a family already overwhelmed with too many children. Her Aunt had managed to get Savannah's sister out of diapers and on to solid food, but that was little comfort with three children still in diapers and needing bottles. Savannah's Aunt was run ragged, but she refused to give up. She knew these children needed a mother even if it was only their Aunt. She lived night and day for these children and they thrived under her care.

The only bright spot in all of this was Savannah's mother's change in attitude. She seemed to come alive after Savannah's birth. Most likely because this was the last pregnancy she would have to endure and she could at last get on with her life. But with four children now in the house, it was impossible for Savannah's mother to be completely free of all responsible for the children.

Her Aunt could not watch and care for four children and complete all the outside errands that needed to be done as well, so Savannah's mother agreed to take over this job herself. It would get her out of the house and away from all the noise and chaos the children created and give her a chance to begin her life again. She loved to shop and socialize and running errands provided the perfect outlet. She would be gone all day shopping, visiting family and friends, and taking the children to their various doctor's appointments. It was amazing how many shots and boosters children their age needed. Not to mention the various colds and sickness they encountered. But one such outing would change her life forever.

She had needed to take Savannah for one of her routine booster shots and check-up. It had been an especially hectic week at the house and her sister-in-law looked as though she was ready to collapse. She knew her sister-in-law needed a break, but she couldn't bring herself to stay home with the three children herself, while her sister-in-law took Savannah to her appointment. She was being selfish she knew, but she didn't care. The thought of taking care of all those children by herself was just too much. Maybe in time she would get used to caring for them, but right now she didn't have the skills to do that. It would be a decisions that would haunt her the rest of her life.

She returned later that day to find her house charred by fire and police and detectives everywhere. It was so badly burnt there was little left of it. The sight of her home in ruins and the possibility of what could have happened left her stunned. She was in such a state of shock, she could neither move, nor scream. She couldn't recall what happened next, only that when she awoke, she was in the hospital being treated by nurses herself.

When she regained enough strength to hear the tale, she had learned that her sister-in-law and all three children had perished in the fire. By the time the fire department had arrived the house was completely engulfed in flames and it was impossible to save anyone. As the police and fire department reviewed the scene it appeared as though something had been cooking on the stove and her sister-in-law had fallen asleep while it cooked. The children had all been down for a nap and no one had a chance to escape. They had all died while still asleep. The sight of the charred bodies, especially those of the children, had been too much for many of the firemen to handle. They had openly wept as the other firemen had struggled with their own grief to remove the bodies.

When Savannah's mother was finally released from the hospital, she went home to live with her parents and try to recover from the terrible tragedy. She was unable to come to terms with what had happened and how her selfishness had brought it all about. She hoped with the loving care of her parents she would one day be able to forgive herself. She knew even now she was being selfish by refusing to live with her husband and help him through his grief, but she had nothing left to give. She felt so empty inside she was of no use to anyone. If it hadn't been for the constant care and attention from her parents, she would have withered up and died.

Her husband wasn't dealing with the grief much better and was blaming himself as well. He should have been able to see how overworked and exhausted his sister had become and demanded that his wife help out more. But he had never been able to refuse his wife anything and was sure doing so would have done very little good anyway. She was determined to do whatever she wanted and cared little what anyone else thought. In his heart he had hoped in time she would change and become the wife and mother he had hoped for. But that had not been the case and now his sister and three of his children had paid with their lives. Because he had been such a weak and powerless person he had allowed his wife to destroy their lives and he was now as accountable for their deaths as she was.

He was so overwhelmed by the thoughts of it all he didn't know where to begin. His wife was living elsewhere, three of his children and his own sister were dead and he had no where to live. He and Savannah were basically homeless, with only the clothes on their backs and the old beat up car he drove to work. It didn't seem like things could get much worse. But he had Savannah to think about and for that reason he needed to go on. He would bury the grief of that day as far down in his soul as he could and hope that he could make something from the rest of his life. He knew Savannah had been spared for a reason and deserved nothing less.

He and Savannah eventually moved in with his mother and siblings and life seemed to improve daily. Savannah's mother visited on occasion and even tried a few times to live with them. But it never seemed to work out for long and she would eventually end up moving back in with her parents. She seemed unable to deal with life on a daily basis and was almost child-like herself. His family was understanding and had tried to help her, but it was no use. She either couldn't or wouldn't deal with family life and finally moved back to her parents place for good.

Savannah didn't miss having her mother around. She had never really known her. The few times she had visited or stayed with them had been more like seeing a distant relative. Her aunts, father and Grandma Amnes were the only family she had ever known and she couldn't have asked for more. They were the loving, caring parents that every child dreams of having. They dotted on her and made her feel very special. She was further blessed by growing up in a working class neighborhood where children were as numerous as pebbles on a beach, assuring her a childhood full of playmates. All in all she felt very lucky with the childhood she had been given.

She could have went on forever just the way things were, but once again life had other plans for her. Plans that would turn her perfect life into a life she would not have wished on her worst enemy. She had often felt different because she had not been given a normal life like the rest of her playmates. A father, mother and siblings. But she was about to realize what a blessing that had been. Life with her mother was far worse than anything she could have imagined.

CHAPTER 3

The call came early one morning as Savannah's father was getting ready for work. Savannah's mother was on the other end and crying so loudly even Savannah could hear her several feet away from the phone. Savannah's father was patiently trying to calm her down, so he could understand what it was she was saying. He finally managed to get the story out of her. Both her parents had died within days of one another and she was all alone trying to sort out her grief. Her father had been struck down several days earlier with a stroke and died within hours. Her mother had followed shortly after, unable to go on without him. Savannah's mother had been so overcome with the tragedy of it all, it had taken her a whole day before she could make the phone call to them. She was now begging Savannah's father to come and live with her in her parents house.

As an only child she would inherit all her parents had, which was quite a sizeable estate. But even with all the money her mother was about to inherit Savannah was not impressed. She had a really bad feeling about this. The few times Savannah's mother had tried to live with them had not worked out well. Her mother was very spoiled and impatient and demanded to be the center of attention.

Insisting everyone within ear shot cater to her every wish. This had made for a very stressful situation to say the least. Savannah had begged her father to let her stay where she was, but her father had not listened. He said that they all belonged together as a family and now that her mother was willing to try again, they could do no less.

He was lonely. Not that he didn't love Savannah, but adults needed other adults as well. Savannah pointed out that he had his mother Grandma Amnes and his siblings to keep him company and they were all very happy together. But her father insisted that the type of company he missed was the love shared between a husband and wife. Something he hoped Savannah's mother would once again share with him. Everything inside of her screamed NO! But she loved her father very much and could not deny him something he obviously wanted very badly. He had always been the best father any child could want and she felt she owed him this much. It would be a decision she would come to regret.

As soon as they moved in with her mother, she wanted to leave. It wasn't that the house and staff weren't nice enough. It was better than anything she could have hoped for. The problem was her mother. She treated them little better than the help. She was mean and spiteful and truly evil when things didn't go her way. Which according to her was most of the time. No one could please her. It didn't matter how hard people tried, her mother was never pleased and would lash out in a minute. Using any means available to show her displeasure.

Her father had found out almost immediately that his dream of living once again as husband and wife was not to be either. She had begun by explaining to her husband that they would be sleeping in separate rooms until she could come to terms with the grief of her parents. But as the months passed and she made no effort to be intimate with him, he realized that this had been just one more of her lies to get what she wanted. By this time he was too embarrassed to return home to his mother's place and admit what a mistake he had made. And in his heart he was still hoping that through some miracle his wife would once again love him the way she had when they had first met and fell in love. Though he would never have admitted it to anyone. What he didn't realize was that his wife had never loved him. She had simply used him the way she used everything she came in contact with.

With Savannah she didn't even try to pretend that she cared for her. She was mean and cruel and spent her time seeing how hateful she could talk to her. She would spend hours while her husband was at work telling Savannah how worthless she was just like her father. That she was ugly and stupid and was penniless except for her. If Savannah had been lucky enough to have someone on her side, they would have pointed out to her that in reality it was actually her mother that was homely and stupid, not her. Her mother was mean and spiteful yes, but not book smart. The only thing her mother said that had any truth to it at all, was that money wise Savannah was at her mercy.

Savannah's mother was wise enough however, not to abuse Savannah around her father. Once Savannah's mother had flew into a rage and beat Savannah within an inch of her life before Savannah's father could separate them. Savannah's father informed his wife if she ever lifted a hand to Savannah again it would be the sorriest day of her life. He loved her very much and would put up with about anything from her, but not the abuse of their daughter. The instant rage in her mother's eyes upon hearing this sent a chill down Savannah's spine. The look in her eyes was so evil, it didn't look human. Savannah knew from that day forward her mother would make her live in Hell when her father was at work and her intuition couldn't have been more correct. She would have told her father about the abuse, but she didn't dare. Once when she threaten to tell, her mother had held her under water in the tub until she turned blue. Telling her next time she would let her drown and tell her father it had been an accident. As evil as her mother was, she believed every word.

She had also threaten the help when they had seen the numerous cuts and bruises on Savannah's arms and legs while dressing her in the mornings for school. But they were as scared of Savannah's mother as she was and the abuse went unreported. The only escape she had from the nightmare she was living, was the time her father was at home and the hours she spent at church.

Her mother had never taken her to church, but her Grandma Amnes and her aunts would come by every Sunday and pick her and her father up to attend church with them. Her father loved attending church and had went with his mother and sister for as long as he could remember. Savannah loved going to church as well. At church she could feel loved and cared for. Something she never felt at home. She learned of a loving and caring God who would protect and care for his children even when the world seemed to desert them. Savannah knew immediately this was a God she wanted to know and share with others who were as abused as she was.

As she grew older she became very active in the church and used prayer as a way to escape her mother's abuse and communicate with a Heavenly father who loved her. This love for God would one day result in her becoming a missionary in an inter-city church helping the homeless and disadvantaged. It didn't matter how cruel and abusive her mother talked about her attending church with her father, she refused to believe what she said. Her mother would go on for hours about how only losers believed in God and all that make believe stuff, but she was too smart for that. It just continued to prove what she had always told Savannah. What a loser she and her father really were! Savannah secretly believed that as evil as her mother was, lightening would probably strike her dead if she ever attempted to enter a church. But she was wise enough to keep that thought to herself.

Savannah also discovered that she was very talented at music and soon began singing and playing an instrument in church. This gave her an opportunity to spend as little time as possible at home. Her father was very proud of her talent and he and his family never missed a chance to watch her perform. He would constantly encourage Savannah's mother to come and watch their little "darling". But Savannah's mother always had a reason why she was unable to attend. After a while it became quite obvious even to him that she just wasn't interested in what Savannah was doing and he stopped asking.

That was fine with Savannah. She really didn't want her mother there anyway. It was enough that her father and his family supported all that she did. But it did supply a means for Savannah to get back at her mother. Savannah realized early on that God had blessed her with many gifts and talents and this was obvious to her mother as well. Savannah realized almost by accident that the more recognition she got for her talents and gifts the crazier it made her mother. Which egged her on to be even more successful. Her mother was finally getting a taste of her own medicine, however small it might be and it made Savannah feel good. She knew getting even was God's job, not hers. But human nature wouldn't let her back down from this small victory.

It was nice seeing someone other than her mother in the limelight. Her mother may have been born rich, but that was all. She had no gifts or talents to speak of and would never be able to compete with Savannah in this area. Savannah knew it and so did her mother and it drove her mother crazy. She would continually tell Savannah that she really wasn't as gifted and talented as people made her believe. They felt sorry for her and were only trying to make her feel better about herself. After years of being beaten down by her mother she almost believed her. But the recognition she was getting from others seemed to be too overwhelming not to be true. So she continued to try to be as successful as she possibly could.

This finally led to her being offered a four year scholarship at a college hundreds of miles away. Savannah jumped at the chance to be out of her mother's house and free from the Hell she had endured at her hands. She would miss her father and his family terribly, but this was a chance she needed to take. She accepted the scholarship and never looked back.

CHAPTER 4

College had been anything but easy. Not coming from a family who had put a lot of stock in education, she didn't know the first thing about what to expect. Her grandfather on her mother's side had accumulated a great deal of wealth, but he had done it the old fashion way-through hard work, not a college education. But Savannah was beginning to realize that education would be her ticket out of a life of poverty and answering to the likes of people like her mother.

Being on a scholarship also helped, because it brought her in constant with scholarship people like herself. Making it much easier to make friends and contacts. Otherwise, unless you were rich or had some other obvious quality you tended to just blend in with the rest of the students. She had not been certain when she started college, what degree she was interested in. But that problem soon took care of itself as well. One of the girls in her current group had been attending a campus youth group and had invited her to attend. Being very interested in religion, she had agreed to go. It would be an event that would change her life.

She knew immediately these were the type of people she was interested in spending the rest of her life with. They were purely good people whose only interest was in helping others and making the world a better place. She had never felt more content and better about herself then when she was in their company. She knew this was what she wanted to do with her life too and decided to complete a degree in ministry. Her hope was to someday work as a missionary in the inter-city. Helping those who had no hope. Her girlfriend Rose had the same interest and they soon became inseparable. Spending all their free time working at homeless shelters and soup kitchens.

It seemed like the four years at college flew by in an instant and before they knew it they had been assigned to their first inter-city job. They had requested to be assigned together and were granted permission. They knew the areas they would be assigned to would be scary at first and wanted each other for support until they felt more at ease with what they were doing. But they could not have imagined just how scary the area they would be working in would be.

When they first arrived at the convent it was surrounded by an eight foot fence, which was kept locked at all times. They were instructed to always go in pairs and to never find themselves alone even for a minute. There was safety in numbers and they could not stress this point to them enough. She wondered to herself if all this security was really necessary, but decided they knew the area better then the two of them and she would do as she was told. After spending several days adjusting to the area, she realized they were not being overly cautious at all. She and Rose were so frightened most of the time they found it difficult to do the assignments they had been given.

The area was something out of a horror movie. It hadn't looked quite so bad when they first came in. But they soon found out that was because they had come in through the best side of the neighborhood. The neighborhood was littered with garbage and trash strewn everywhere. Young people seemed to roam the streets aimlessly and the older people spent their time setting on their stoops watching the traffic and people go by. Each house had a gated fence around the lawn and it was locked at all times. Even while the owners were seated on the front steps. Drugs were sold on the street corners in broad daylight with no one stopping them. Gun fire rang out throughout the day, with police and ambulances a constant sight. The area was so chaotic she and Rose had no idea where to begin.

Their assignment was to reach the young people of the community and start a youth program at the convent's community center. The convent and church took up most of the block, with a community center and food kitchen located next to the church. It was really a very compact little community within itself and there would not have been a reason to go outside the walls if it hadn't been their desire to reach the community for Christ and give the youth a safer more desirable neighborhood to live in.

They began each morning with prayer and depended on God to give them direction and safety for the day. The nuns were sure to remember them in their daily prayers as well. Even though they were living at the convent with the nuns they were not part of the Catholic Church. They were an independent Christian organization that included all Protestant faiths. They had teamed up with the nuns of the convent for safety reasons and because the nuns had indicated that there was available space for them to use. Their organization would coordinate their activities with the nuns plans for the day, so that the same areas of the compound would not be used at the same time. This was a great operation for both organizations as it provided safety in numbers and additional revenues.

The nuns were finding it very difficult to manage financially in this area. They had begun with a sizeable amount of money for their ministry in this neighborhood, but as the area continued to be taken over by drugs and crime the money for their programs had been eaten up at an alarming rate. They were hoping with the combined efforts of another missionary group they would be able to combine resources and win back the community for the people. As this was Savannah's organization's goal as well, they were only too happy to join forces with the nuns. It was a monumental task for both organizations and they would need all the available resources they could find to save this neighborhood and to keep the convent financially afloat.

She and Rose had no idea where to begin their ministry in this neighborhood, so they began with the basics. As litter strewn as the neighborhood was, they decided this would be a good place to start. They began the morning with a box of plastic trash bags, work gloves and T-shirts that identified who they were. The organization they worked for "God's Warriors" explained how important it was to have some identification as to who they were. In a neighborhood such as this, the people were very aware of who belonged there and who didn't. Being new to the area, it was important that Savannah and Rose identify who they were right from the beginning.

They had both been issued T-shirts, in various colors, when they were given this assignment. Each T-shirt read,

"God's Warriors-Reaching Communities for Christ." In this way the T-shirts served two purposes. It identified who they were and what their purpose for being there was. It was also a non threatening way of letting the neighborhood know that they were there to serve them. As time went by they hoped those in the community would feel comfortable approaching them. In the meantime they would keep a low profile and do what they could to begin improving the neighborhood.

This first task took a real act of faith. Savannah had seen garbage and trash before, but nothing like this. This was the most disgusting thing she had ever seen. The garbage and trash had been there so long that maggots had begun growing on it. Rats the size of small cats were everywhere and stray animals were eating the eatable parts of the fresher garbage. She was sure the rats and stray animals carried some life threatening disease and prayed she wouldn't be bit. She and Rose had needed to pray constantly that morning while they worked just to continue. The sight and smell of the garbage and trash was overwhelming. They tried not to breathe too deeply as they worked. That would have been the beginning of the end. Shallow breathing was almost too much to take at times.

The morning had gone by quite quickly. Drawing a small crowd of onlookers who were trying to figure out who these crazy people were cleaning up their neighborhood and why. No one approached them, but no one seemed in a hurry to leave either. Once noon approached they returned to the convent for lunch. But after the disgusting sights and smells of the morning, they decided to skip eating and just rest during the lunchtime period. They would soon be returning to garbage duty and they didn't need their lunch coming up as they worked. Just keeping water down would be a big enough problem. But they felt this was where God had led them and they were determined to make it work no matter how disgusting the assignments were.

The organization was pretty open as to how each person went about completing their assignments. Everyone met in the morning for breakfast at 7:00 a.m. At 7:30 a meeting was held and each person described their plans for the day, area they would be working in and partner they would be working with. Each team was also given a cell phone with a two way pager system that connected directly to the convent. Assuring that they would have contact with the organization at all times. A life line of sorts to ensure as much safety as possible. They would then meet for lunch at noon and then resume work at one. Ending the work day at 5:00 p.m. and meeting for supper at 6:00 p.m. At 7:00 p.m. they would all meet again and explain how their assignments had gone, any problems that had arisen and any help or supplies they might need for the next day. A prayer meeting would follow at 8:00 p.m. and lights were normally out by 10:00 p.m. There was little free time even on the weekends. But they hadn't expected a life of ease. They were here to serve God.

The trash pick-up and removal went on for several days. They would fill the bags with the trash and garbage and then take the bags back to the convent to dispose of. After a while the neighborhood residence seemed to lose interest in what they were doing and faded away. They found that a few people from time to time would stop and help for a while, but nothing on a regular basis. Then something rather funny happened. Several mothers who had houses full of kids realized that by sending their children out to help Savannah and Rose during the day they could get free babysitting service. They weren't really interested in any spiritual help or guidance the two of them may offer, they were just glad to have a break away from all those kids. This was just the opportunity Savannah and Rose were looking for. They were pretty sure why the mothers had allowed the kids to help them, but they didn't care. They would use the opportunity to share Christ with them and show them a different kind of life. One filled with love and hope from a Heavenly Father.

They sang church songs as they worked. Ones Savannah and Rose had sung themselves in Sunday School while growing up. They also recounted their favorite Bible stories as the children worked. It wasn't long before the group had most of the trash and garbage in the neighborhood picked up and had moved on to painting over the graffiti that was everywhere-bridges, public buildings, neighborhood fences, stop signs. You name it and it most likely had graffiti on it. But with the group they had accumulated, about twelve kids in all, the work went quite fast.

Savannah and Rose, had begun bringing refreshments to the work site for the kids. The inter-city could be really hot and dirty in the summer and the kids were always running home to get a drink or something to eat. By bringing refreshments to the site, this eliminated the need for them to go home. Savannah and Rose had also gone to each of the children's homes and asked permission to take the children back to the convent each day for lunch. The mother's had been only too happy to give permission.

This in itself opened up even more opportunities to

reach the children. Most of them had never been inside a convent, met a nun or even attended church. They seemed rather fascinated by this new world they had discovered. A world safe from the violence and crime they lived with daily. Most of the children began attending the Sunday School program offered at the convent on Sunday's and Savannah and Rose had given new Bibles to each of them with their names engraved on the front right corner of the cover. They had also ordered T-shirts for all of the children to wear while they worked. The shirts were similar to Savannah and Rose's with one exception. Instead of stating "God's Warriors-Reaching Communities for Christ." Theirs stated, "God's Little Warriors-Reaching Communities for Christ." The kids loved the T-shirts and wore them like a badge of honor.

They were getting so many kids now that they had, had to pass some of them off to other members of their organization. They had set up work stations of a sort and the children could choose which area they wanted to work in for the day. There was still the trash, garbage and graffiti station that Savannah and Rose ran, but they had also added visitation to the elderly and shut-ins which was headed by two other leaders. A bible study and choir group was also offered from 3:00-5:00p.m. for any child who wished to attend. The programs were making quite a stir in the neighborhood and the residence seemed to appreciate them being there. It was a lot of hard work, but one of the most rewarding jobs they had ever done.

CHAPTER 5

Things couldn't have been going better, when the violence of the community struck home. There was always the fear of violence in this community, including the numerous gangs that were everywhere. It took up a great deal of Savannah and Rose's time each day securing the safety of the children that were in their care. It was imperative that the children could be accounted for at all times. Anyone wandering away from the group was immediately sent back to the convent for the day. A few minutes alone in this community was all it took for tragedy to strike. But it would be an event much bigger than that, that would shake their world.

They were working on the garbage and trash detail one day when gunfire rang out. As instructed, the children immediately dropped to the ground and huddled together for safety. When the gunfire had stopped and the children got up to begin working again they discovered a grisly site. One of the gang members had been shot and was bleeding profusely. Several other gang members had been shot as well, but this one was the most badly injured. Savannah and Rose were afraid if they waited for the ambulance to arrive it might be too late for him. His pulse was already very weak and his breathing was almost nonexistent. It was decided in that split second, that Rose would return to the convent with the children and Savannah would drive the victim to the hospital in the van. It took several minutes before Savannah and Rose could manage to load him into the van. They were both fairly strong, but the victim was a good size man and dead weight due to his injuries.

Many of the children were crying and hugging each other for comfort. Savannah had hoped to shield the children from ever seeing this kind of violence up close, but she knew there was a good chance it would one day happen. She had to keep taking deep breaths herself, just to keep from fainting. It was one of the grisliest sites she had ever seen and something she was ill prepared for. Growing up in a small town she had never been exposed to this kind of violence. But she knew if she hoped to make a difference in this community she would have to get use to it.

When she arrived at the hospital, the staff was amazed that she and her girlfriend had been able to load this man into the van. He was barely holding on to life when she arrived and the staff was unsure whether they would be able to save him or not. It wasn't long before the police and detectives arrived at the emergency room to get a statement from her. She knew giving a statement would be risky and might put the convent and herself in harms way. But if she didn't help the police, the violence would just continue and probably escalate.

It was only gang members involved this time, but it could have just as easily been innocent bystanders instead. She was here to help the community and she knew she needed to do whatever was necessary to stop this senseless violence. The children she worked with deserved to live in a neighborhood free from crime and violence and it was up to her to stand up for them. She wished she could have left the identification up to someone else, but she and Rose had clearly seen the incident and she was sure no one else would step forward to help the police.

When Savannah arrived back at the convent, she found out that the violence had continued. She would never forgive herself for leaving Rose alone to return the children to the convent. At the time she and Rose were only thinking of saving the man who had been wounded. Never realizing that those who had shot him would be laying in ambush for them. But that is exactly what had happened.

As Rose was returning the children to the convent, one of the shooters stepped out from an abandon building and began assaulting her. She had screamed at the children to run for the safety of the convent, holding the attacker off as they did. When the children arrived at the convent they had told the leaders what had happened and the leaders had returned to the area to retrieve Rose, but it had been too late.

When they got there Rose was barely breathing. She had been so badly beaten it was hard to tell who she was. She had numerous stab wounds to her upper body and face and was laying in a pool of blood. The leaders begged her to hang on, but she was so badly injured she wouldn't survive. The emergency medical team had arrived minutes after being called and started work on Rose immediately. But she died before they could transport her to the hospital.

Savannah was so devastated by what had happened that she was unable to get out of bed for days. She just lay there while Rose's family was contacted and arrangements were made for her funeral. Savannah was so racked by guilt that she prayed God would take her life as well. She had made a tragic decision and now because of her, her best friend was dead. She couldn't live with what she had done.

She had chosen to save the life of a gang member at the expense of her best friend. She knew that they were not to be alone, no matter what the circumstances. How could she have been so stupid as to believe that this once wouldn't matter? How many times had she and Rose explained this exact thing to the children they were in charge of?! She now doubted everything about herself. If she could have made such a tragic decision once, what was to keep her from putting other people's life in danger again?

She had really believed this was where God had wanted her and these were the people God had sent her to help. But now she questioned even that. It was because of who Rose was, that Savannah had managed to become all that she was. Rose was so pure and holy that Savannah had wanted to be just like her. But now she had managed to destroy all that. She had killed the best friend she ever had.

The nuns and the team she was working for tried to comfort her. Tried to explain that it was her love for all God's people that had caused this tragedy and that Rose had believed in what they were doing as well. Evil had brought about this sad day, but they had to work beyond this tragedy and not let evil win out. It was what Rose would have wanted and it was what they needed to do. But Savannah wasn't so sure. She was so broken hearted it was difficult to think clearly. All she wanted to do right now was to run away from this place and find a safe comfortable place that was free from such violence.

She did however, stick around long enough to identify

several suspects the detectives tracked down. With her positive identification and the skin fibers they had found under Rose's finger nails when doing her autopsy, they were able to put the suspects away for life. But it was little consolation to her. Her best friend was still dead and the scum that killed her was still alive. Alive to possibly be released on a technicality or by some scum bag lawyer who would argue that he deserved another chance because of the poor upbringing he'd had.

What bothered Savannah most about what happened, other than the death of Rose, was how jaded she now felt toward her fellow man. She once had an innocent and naive attitude, believing that with God's help and enough love anyone could be saved. She no longer believed that. She was so changed by what had happened, she now believed that evil people needed to be separated from the good ones. God could change anybodies heart, but that was no longer her job. She would concentrate on saving the ones who wanted to be saved and leave the rest to God. If they chose to burn in Hell, so be it. At least they wouldn't bring the rest of mankind down with them.

Her faith had been shaken to the core and she needed time to heal from the wounds. She had asked for a one month leave of absence from her job at the convent to try and regroup. To find a renewed spirit for caring and a way to let Rose's memory live through her work. She wasn't sure if one month would be enough. Only time would tell. But she still had enough faith left that she hoped her heart would heal and she could still make something good out of her life. She hoped this event wouldn't prove to destroy her and all that she might have become.

God willing she would live to fight another day and become more than she could have hoped for. But right now all she could manage to do was survive from one day to the next. That would be her goal for the month. Once the healing began she hoped she would be able to understand the reason such a tragic event was allowed to happen. But that too may never be understood and she would need to find closure, even if she couldn't find answers. That was the only way she would be able to move forward with her life.

CHAPTER 6

Savannah returned to her hometown, but not to her parents place. She decided to spend the time she had with her Grandma Amnes. She was really old now and there would be very little time left to share with her. Her father stopped by often to see her, but her mother never came. She was supposedly offended because Savannah had chosen to live at Grandma Amnes, instead of with them. Savannah knew this was just an excuse by her mother not to visit, which was fine with her. They both hated each other and there was no reason to pretend otherwise.

The abuse Savannah had suffered at her mother's hands could never be forgiven or forgotten. She had prayed for the strength to forgive her, but the hatred was just too strong. And in all fairness, the abuse had never stopped. She still found the time to contact Savannah at the convent just to remind her what a worthless, hateful child she was. Demanding that she return home and care for her and their home the way a good child would. But Savannah was not about to fall for the guilt her mother was trying to lay on her. She had escaped her "den of horrors" once and she wasn't about to revisit it again.

Savannah was sure her mother did miss her. She had

been her unpaid servant and punching bag for years and now she had no one to abuse but her husband. And the abuse she reaped on Savannah's father could not have been more evident. He was now an old and broken man. So beaten down by her that he spent his days avoiding her and life in general. He was a shell of a man with no spirit or soul left. It was pitiful to see what he had become and it made Savannah's hatred of her mother even stronger.

She missed the father he had once been and it enraged her that her mother had the power to completely destroy another human being. It further enraged her that her father could not see her mother for the evil villain she was. He continued to believe that somewhere within her soul there existed a heart. Even though life continued to prove otherwise.

He just couldn't seem to believe that someone he had loved and spent most of his life with could be that evil and uncaring. It seemed easier for him to believe the lie, than to admit the truth. She felt sorry for her father, but she was not about to allow her mother to destroy her life the way she had his. She could clearly see her mother for who she was and intended to stay as far away from her as possible.

Savannah hadn't been home long before she ran into an old classmate, Edward Brooks. She hadn't really known him that well in school. He had come from the wrong side of the tracks and was rumored to have had a very dysfunctional family. Though no one could really explain in what way the family was dysfunctional. They either didn't know or weren't talking about it. But if people had really known what type of family Savannah had been raised in they probably would have considered her family dysfunctional too.

Whatever the dysfunction was, he seemed fine to her. In fact he reminded her of her father when she was young. There seemed to be a goodness and caring about him that instantly melted her heart. He was not what you would call good looking, but he wasn't unpleasant to look at either. He'd been rather heavy as a child, but now had a slim, muscular physique. She couldn't help noticing how personable and carefree he was, with an infectious smile that made you want to smile right back.

After a few minutes of conversation he asked her if she would like to go out with him on Saturday night, if she wasn't seeing someone else. He knew he was being rather forward, but he had always liked her and would like to get to know her better. She immediately agreed. She hadn't really noticed him that much in school, but she could see now that she had made a mistake. He was someone she thought would be enjoyable to know.

She wasn't really looking for someone right now, but if she had been, he would have been a perfect choice. She would go out with him as friends and see where the relationship went. If nothing else, they could keep each other company. If things went really well, well who knew! But that was a ways down the road yet and there was also her work to consider. But she was getting the cart before the horse. They hadn't even went out on a date yet! So there was no telling what might happen. She needed to take it one step at a time and not try to live life before it happened.

But she needn't have worried about how the date would go. Edward had every intention of making the evening as unforgettable as he could. He couldn't believe that Savannah had actually agreed to go out with him and he would do anything to make sure she would continue to date him. He would finally be the envy of all his friends and after a lifetime of scorn that knowledge was sweet.

But his friends had laughed hysterically when he had told them he had asked out Savannah Richards. When they finally stopped laughing, they had advised him to save himself the embarrassment and heartache she would eventually cause him and just forget about it. But he had no intention of forgetting about it. She was an opportunity of a lifetime and he was going to do all he could to make sure it didn't end.

He had never been shy about going after what he wanted and this was not going to be the exception. He had been a social outcast most of his life and had, to fight for most of what he had gotten. He had never been lucky enough to date someone as special as Savannah. He normally dated women who had as much trouble getting dates as he did. Someone as popular and pretty as Savannah never looked his way. He was invisible to them. But not this time.

His luck was changing and right now he felt like the luckiest man alive. She had been the prettiest girl in school and there wasn't a man alive who didn't want to date her. But unlike other girls who had the same kind of looks, she didn't have the ego that went with it. It was almost as though she didn't realize she was pretty. He had also heard she was devotedly religious which further surprised him. In what little he knew about pretty girls, they were mostly party girls. But not this one. She didn't drink, smoke or do drugs and refused to be around anyone who did.

He knew this last part might be a bit of a challenge for him, because he had never been raised in the church himself. His family had went to church on Easter Sunday and Christmas like most families did, but not during the rest of the year. He was known to do a little drinking himself, but only among his friends. It wasn't something that was general knowledge, but his relatives did have a reputation for being hell raisers, especially among the men in the family. He had tried to keep a low profile in this area, because he realized that families like Savannah's would not allow someone with a wild reputation to date their daughters and these were the type of women he had always dreamed of dating. He may not have been brought up among the more acceptable families in the community, but he sure wanted to marry into them.

Savannah was a little surprised at the bad reputation Edward's family and relatives had in the community. They were known as the "Bad Boy's" in town and no self respecting family would allow their children, girls or boys, to date the family. But Savannah had not seen this in Edward. It was true she didn't know the family very well, but in all the time she had spent with him she had never seen him act in any way other than polite and respectful. She knew that several of his cousins were known to be on the wild side and it had landed them in trouble with the law. Nothing too serious, but it did nothing to endear them to the community.

As time went on and these situations with his relatives continued to happen, Edward had explained that these cousins were considered the "black sheep" of the family and didn't represent how the family really was. His mother and sisters were very religious and they had nothing to do with that side of the family. His mother kept a strong hand on the family and tried to bring them up right.

Savannah had no way of knowing this early in the relationship, that most of what he said was a lie. It was true that his mother wanted the children to be thought well of in the community, but she had worked so many hours when they were growing up that she rarely saw them. The only time she really interacted with them, was when they had gotten themselves into trouble in her absence and she needed to deal with the consequences and straighten them out. Otherwise, they basically raised themselves. Something Savannah would find out later, was similar to the way she was raised, minus the abuse.

CHAPTER 7

Edward's mother had come from a family that was all about appearances, but lacked any substance. Nearly the same way his father had been raised. His mother's father had been an ordained minister in the deep South and had been highly regarded by most who knew him. But he lived a far different life than the one he showed to the world. He had a dark side to him and was far worse acting behind closed doors than many of the sinners he preached to each Sunday.

He kept his shy, timid wife constantly pregnant. Resulting in a house overflowing with children and a wife too old before her time. He also kept a mistress on the side who was willing to indulge his insatiable appetite for bizarre sexual acts. Even though many of the things he asked her to do went against every instinct she had and were very painful to perform. But she knew how much he appreciated her willingness to indulge his fantasies, by how loving and caring he was afterwards. No matter how sadistic and painful their lovemaking may be for her, he would always kiss her and gently rock her until the pain subsided. With tear filled eyes he would tell her how much he needed and adored her. How he only felt alive when they were together, sharing their passion with one another.

His wife was such a cold fish, he said, that she would never pleasure him the way she could. He knew how much she loved him too by how willing and giving she was in pleasing him. Never objecting to anything he asked. He would never let her go. She was his whole world. The only one who understood him. Understood why he needed to do the things he did.

He managed to keep her a secret by seeing her during the time he was scheduled to do visitations. As a minister it was his job to do visitations in the community and get to know the people. Helping them with any problems or spiritual needs they might have. But the only visitations he was doing now, was with his mistress. Having marathon sex with her until they were both exhausted. Sometimes lasting well into the night.

His wife seemed none the wiser. Being constantly pregnant and raising a house full of children, she had little time to think of anything else. She rarely left the house and when she did it was only to attend church. As the minister's wife, she was expected to be there every Sunday. She had recently found out she was pregnant again and wasn't sure she could handle any more. Her body was deteriorating at an alarming rate and she could barely go on.

Her husband had noticed it too and offered to bring a woman in to help her. The woman was pregnant too and needed a place to stay after her husband had left her. His wife was shocked, but pleased he had been so thoughtful in finding her some help. But she had no way of knowing that this woman was her husband's pregnant mistress. He had just found out days earlier that his mistress was pregnant too and he had no intentions of leaving her on her own. He had planned on this being a temporary solution, but to his disgust she was as fertile as his wife.

Many in the community wondered what was really going on in their house. But no one wanted to believe that a -man of God- could be doing anything wrong. Edward's grandmother hadn't questioned it at first either. But slowly she began to notice how her husband hovered over her with a protectiveness she couldn't remember him ever showing her. She was suppose to be there to help her out, but her husband refused to let her tire herself. Afraid that the strain might hurt the baby. When she asked him about her own pregnancy, he answered by saying she had given birth to so many children already nothing could harm her. She was livid with him, but kept her feelings to herself.

When the woman's child was born she had her answer. There was no denying who the father was. The baby looked just like all her babies had. In fact it could have been a twin to the one she had just given birth to. When she brought this up to her husband, he went into a rage and beat her so badly she wondered if she would survive. He was screaming at her to never accuse him of such a vile thing again or he would make sure he killed her next time.

But when the woman managed to become pregnant again shortly after giving birth, she knew for sure it could be none other than her husband's. He tried to blame the new pregnancy on the woman's ex-husband. Saying that they had met several times since the birth of her child trying to get back together. But soon realized it was hopeless and gave up trying. Only for her to then realize she was pregnant again. But Edward's Grandmother knew this was a lie. Since the woman had moved in, Edward's Grandfather had been less interested in her.

Prior to that, he had demanded sex from her everyday. Even when she was much to sick to accommodate him. But she knew if she didn't he would beat her and make her have sex with him anyway. Making the act as painful and cruel as he could to teach her a lesson. It was just easier to comply. But shortly after the woman arrived he had suggested she move out of their bedroom, to another room, just until she could get her strength back. This really surprised her, because he had never suggested such a thing in the past. But when she heard loud muffled noises coming from his bedroom several nights later, she began to understand why.

When she heard the noises, she had gotten up to investigate what was going on and seen her husband in the act of pleasuring the other woman. When he noticed her standing there he gave her an evil smirk and continued kissing and caressing the other woman. With a tenderness the two of them had never shared. She had been temporarily frozen to the spot, unable to take her eyes off them. But as he continued on with the woman, performing graphic sexual acts with her, she fled in horror. This final act of cruelty sucked the life from her.

When the other woman went on to give birth yet again, Edward's Grandmother lost her will to live. As she lay in bed, too weak and beaten down to move, her husband entertained the other woman as though she were the wife. He spent everyday with her. Running errands in town together and leaving her children home for Edward's mother and siblings to watch. When they returned home, they would be laughing and whispering to each other as though they shared some special secret together. Oblivious to anyone around them.

When Edward's mother had finally had enough, she braved her father's wrath by asking him why they had to care for the woman's children while she spent all day with him. He went into another rage, much like he had with their mother. Informing her and the rest of the family that he was in charge and would make the decisions in the family. Not them! They were to do exactly as they were told and never question anything he said or did again.

It became obvious to them at that moment, she was not really the housekeeper, but their father's lover. That would explain the sounds they had also heard coming from their father's room late at night and the reason their mother hadn't gotten pregnant again. But his lover wasn't having any trouble staying pregnant. As each new pregnancy appeared, he would continue to explain them away as her failed attempt to reconcile with her ex-husband. But they knew his story was a lie, just as their mother had, because she was never out of their father's sight long enough to meet with anyone else.

But they were forced to keep up the lie anyway. Knowing that their lives wouldn't be worth living if they told anyone what was really going on. It broke their hearts to see their mother waste away and finally end her own life. She had been the only bright spot in their otherwise miserable life. They were sure the doctor who had been called to pronounce her dead knew too. But he was kind enough to rule the death an accident. Sparing them and their father the shame of having the whole world know their mother had committed suicide.

But after their mother died and their father married the

woman within months, it was hard to fool anyone. There were even a few raised eyebrows one Sunday in church when he made the announcement of his upcoming marriage to her. Explaining to them that it only seemed logical, given the number of children he was now responsible for taking care of. She had been their housekeeper and knew the children well. She was such a kind and loving woman, she had agreed to take on their care. He nervously laughed as he added that few women would be brave enough to take on such a task. But as the congregation eyed her swollen belly, nearly ready to burst, they wondered if it didn't involve something far different.

She had managed to give birth as often as their mother had. A year didn't go by without her dropping another baby. But unlike their mother, she wasn't expected to care for them or do anything around the house. Her only job was to please their father and be his constant companion. He was so preoccupied with her he barely knew the rest of them existed. The only time he bothered with them was when he needed something or his wife was angry with him.

But lately there seemed to be a strain in the marriage they hadn't seen before. Their stepmother was again pregnant, but instead of their father being pleased he seemed annoyed. What they didn't know was their father had demanded his wife have no more children after the last birth. He had told her she was beginning to look old and haggard and was losing all her looks. Her once beautiful face was puffy and lined and her beautiful figure was as thick as two saddlebags tied to her waist and hips. He had cruelly remarked, if she didn't stop hatching kids out year after year she would soon be as big as a house and as fat and ugly as his wife had been.

He knew a hill lady that had all kinds of potions to prevent pregnancies and end those that had started. If she wanted to stay with him, as his lover, she would make sure she used them. Otherwise she would just be a baby factory like his wife and he would only have sex with her to relieve himself. As a minister, his wife was suppose to give birth often and he would accommodate her in this way, but nothing more. He would find a new, fresh lover for all the fantasies he had in mind and she would be the one sleeping with him and receiving all his attention, not her.

She had done all that he ask and more, but she had still found herself pregnant once again. She had tried to hide the pregnancy from him as long as she could. But before long he had noticed the all familiar signs of a new pregnancy. He had went into a rage and demanded she rid herself of this pregnancy. But by this time the pregnancy was too far along and nothing could be done. She tried to calm him down by begging him to show her what she could do to make him love her again. She would do anything, no matter how strange or bizarre it might be. He was more than happy to play out his demented sex acts with her until he found someone new. But of course he didn't share this information with her.

They continued their pleasures in the bedroom till all hours of the morning. But to her the tenderness they once shared seemed to be gone. He didn't seem as caring and attentive to her as he had always been. She had thought they had patched up their differences, but she wasn't so sure now. She had even allowed him to enter her from behind, using the back opening instead of the normal opening, when she had become so large that having sex any other way was nearly impossible. But as she neared her delivery date, he began leaving her home more and more. Going so far as to move her out of his bedroom and into his former wife's room.

When he showed up several weeks later with a young girl, barely in her teens, they all knew she was his new "housekeeper". Their stepmother would now hear the muffled noises coming from her husband's room, just as their mother had. Watch this young teen take her place as the lady of the house and in sick fascination watch as she satisfied her husband's insatiable sexual appetite. Witness him holding and caressing her after he had satisfied his lust for sadistic and violent love making on her. Not caring who might be watching. Watch her become bloated with child soon after her arrival and the tender way her husband now heaped attention on her. The way he used to care for her.

After she had given birth, she tried to work her way back into his life. Once again offering to do anything he wanted, so long as he would love her again. But he wasn't interested. He now had a 13 year old "housekeeper" that was willing to satisfy him as she once had. She was so young, energetic and fresh. Not fat and bloated from a lifetime of childbirth. Looking at his wife now, against his young and innocent lover repulsed him. He would never touch his wife again or have anything to do with her and the children they had sired together. And he wasn't shy about telling her so.

His wife was devastated, but unwilling to end her life as his first wife had. She would leave him and her children behind and start life again. She had a sister who lived on the west coast and first thing tomorrow she would load up her things in their car and head west to live with her. She would forget this part of her life ever existed and never look back.

CHAPTER 8

By this time Edward's mother and siblings had, had enough. Their stepmother leaving had helped some, but now their father was starting the process all over again with the new "housekeeper". She was already showing signs of being pregnant and no wonder. They spent most of their time locked in his bedroom. Making enough noise to wake up the whole house.

Her father had recently been suspended from his job, when he had decided to bring the young "housekeeper" home. Word had gotten out and the church could no longer cast a blind eye to him. He would be suspended until they could investigate the situation further and clear him of any wrong doing.

He went into a rage. Cursing and accusing them of having an evil mind to think that he would be doing anything other than helping the poor girl out. Coming from a poor family as she did, with too many mouths to feed. Her father had given her to him. He was to provide her with room and board and she would help out around the house. But when a few of the church members saw her out in the yard one day and noticed how bloated around the middle she had become, they told him they felt it was time for him to go.

He had been so enraged at first, he could barely speak. So stunned he hadn't noticed the lady standing next to him. She said she was very sorry over what had just happened. She hadn't meant to ease drop, but it was hard not to hear what they were saying and she thought she might be able to help him. She wanted to apologize in advance, if what she was about to say was offensive to him.

She couldn't help notice lately what a struggle it seemed to be for him to raise his numerous children, now that his wife had passed away and his new wife was pregnant herself. (No one knew yet that she had already delivered her baby and left him). She could only imagine the financial and emotional stress it must be causing him. She knew children were a gift from God and he seemed to have been overly blessed. But as blessed as he was, there were others in the world who had not been as blessed.

They prayed daily for a child they could adopt and call their own. They would lavish them with love and possessions a father like himself could never do. These children would want for nothing and the adopted parents would pay the families generously for their children. When she discreetly mentioned how generous, he was stunned. But he regained his composer before she noticed.

She told him she would give him some time to think it over and get back with him. But he wasn't about to let this opportunity slip through his hands. He told her he had been trying to figure out a way to take care of them all, but was failing miserably. She was an answer to prayer. He couldn't think of a better gift to give his children, than allowing them to be adopted by such loving couples. But she would have to be discreet and make sure no one found out.

She told him he didn't need to worry, she had been at this a long time and no one was ever the wiser. The couples demanded complete secrecy too and these rich clients didn't want to know where the children came from or who their families were. She was very discreet about what she did and would be out of business if she wasn't. These were private adoptions, so there was no reason to worry about anyone finding out.

Assured his secret would be kept, he told her he had four children under the age of five that could be adopted. Her face broke into a wide smile and she said with that many children to be adopted he could expect to be very comfortable financially. However she would need to pick the children up immediately. He assured her it would be no problem. He was as anxious to place them in a good home, as she was to get them. The final price she quoted him was more money than he had ever dreamed of. She told him she would also be willing to buy anymore "accidents" he might have as well, looking directly at the young teen standing beside him. He winked at her and said they had a deal. He would call her as soon as the baby was born.

He had no idea having children could be so profitable. He was beginning to feel all his troubles fade away. He would soon be on easy street and living the good life. He was more than happy to let these children go. They were his ex-mistress/wife's children and with her gone and the children to be adopted immediately, all memory of her would soon be erased. He had never liked children anyway. It was the sex he had enjoyed. Children were always screaming and crying and driving him crazy. He also didn't want his new "housekeeper" saddled with a new born. He had much better plans in mind for her.

He would have to come up with some kind of story to explain to the older children where their younger siblings had gone. Then the case would be closed. Truth be told, they would probably be glad some of their burden had been lifted. Either way it didn't matter. The younger children were going and he would soon be a happy, wealthy man. Heck he might even reconsider and let his "housekeeper" have a few more babies for him to cash in on.

She was young enough to bounce back quickly without losing any of her looks or beautiful body. She should be able to have another two or three babies, without much damage. He would make sure she ate a very limited diet after the babies were born, until she got her slim, boylike figure back. He liked his partners to have unnaturally thin bodies, that looked very child like in appearance. If she was unable to get her looks back, there were always other young girls to choose from. Coming from families like his young "housekeeper", who couldn't afford to keep them and would lend them out in exchange for room and board.

Of course the families would have no idea what kind of housework he was really having them do and by the time they did, it would be too late. They were way too poor to take care of a daughter and baby too. They would be enraged over the way he had treated them, but there was nothing they could do. With the amount of money he had, the girls would be eager to be chosen by him and their families would realize he could provide a better home for them, than they could. If they happened to have a few "accidents" along the way, while they were with him, it would just be more money in his pockets. In fact he just might encourage them to have several "accidents" for all the extra money it would bring him. It was a win-win situation for him all the way around.

But for now he would just enjoy the "housekeeper" he already had. She was so much fun for him there was no way he was ready to let her go for now. He enjoyed her so much more than he ever remembered enjoying his wife or mistress. The only drawback was her age. She was so young and tender that the things he wanted to do with her were so painful she would end up crying in agony. Unable to stand the pain. But he found by giving her several glasses of moonshine each day, she would become glassy eyed and relaxed. Allowing him to do anything he wanted with her.

He made sure he kept her as intoxicated as he dared. Never allowing her to sober up. She was putty in his hands when she was drunk and anything he could imagine, she was eager to do for him. If he died today, he couldn't die any happier. She was better than anything he could have hoped for. But he had no way of knowing his evil life was about to end.

His "housekeeper" had managed to sober up enough one day to go outside for a breath of fresh air, just as her brothers were walking by. Alarmed by her very rounded belly, they stopped to ask her who had done that to her. She told them not to worry, everything was ok. The man papa had given her to had explained that as her guardian it was his responsibility to show her what it was to be a woman and how to please a man so he would never leave her.

She had been afraid at first, but he had helped her relax by giving her several glasses of alcohol. Once she felt warm inside and began dozing off from all the alcohol, he had laid her on the bed and began piercing her with something that sent stabbing pains surging through her body. It had seemed like a very hazy dream at first, as she tried to move away from him. But she was unable to do anything because of all the alcohol he had given her. He had pinned her down with his body so she couldn't move. Continuing to send the stabbing pains through her body until he had satisfied himself. Then he began again, gentler this time, making her repeat the process with him over and over again until she had gotten it just right. Then he proceeded to show her how to pleasure a man.

He had said that most "father figures" would only take time to show her the basics. But he felt it was important for her to know everything there was to pleasing a man, including oral pleasures, which men liked most. He told her not to be afraid. He would take very good care of her. He didn't enjoy showing her all this stuff either, but as her "father" he was required to teach her and he wanted to make sure he did the best job he could.

It had been hard for her at first because she didn't know anything about it. But he was so patient with her. Never losing his temper or scolding her. He would just patiently have her repeat each procedure again and again. Each time guiding her body and head with his hands until she was exactly in the position he wanted. He had instructed her this way every day since she had gotten here and she had learned a lot.

In fact she had progressed so well that he had shown her some special positions only his very best students got to learn. She had, had to drink extra alcohol to learn these lessons however, because the pain was even more intense than the first lessons had been. It was so painful she couldn't keep from crying out. He had told her it was alright to cry out. She just wasn't very good at it yet, but they would keep on practicing. Soon she would be so good she would barely notice the pain. She just needed to try a little harder.

It was only because she was his favorite student that he had bothered to show her these special positions. He said she made him so happy when she tried really hard and got it right. She felt really happy too, that she had been able to please him and make him proud of her. When he was really proud of her he would buy her a bag of sugary candy as a reward and let her eat it all by herself. Not making her share it with the other children. When she was extra good he would buy her the little dolls she really liked and the see-through nighties, in such pretty colors, that he liked. She loved the candy and little dolls she could sleep with at night and it made her want to try even harder.

They practiced these new positions day and night until she had gotten accustomed to the extreme pain. But she didn't mind any more because she knew she would get more of the special gifts she liked so much. But he had warned her that once a baby started to grow inside of her, they could no longer use the first opening he had shown her, because it might hurt the baby. That was just how thoughtful he was, she said. He had told her they would have to use the opening further back to continue their lessons. She didn't need to be afraid of the pain because it was natural. He promised to give her all the alcohol she needed, but cautioned her that this was the most important position she needed to learn.

Her husband would insist on using this position to

safeguard their baby when she was pregnant and expect her to use it after the baby was born to prevent her from getting pregnant again. He had said that husbands didn't want their wife's pregnant all the time and would leave them for other women if they did. Sure enough, as soon as she missed her period he began using the second opening exclusively to protect the baby, just as he promised he would. He told her he was very disappointed that she had allowed herself to get pregnant at all. But he would forgive her just this one. After all she was just learning and didn't know any better. But they could never allow this to happen again.

He had only shown her the first opening, so she could see what terrible things happened if she used it. He said he knew she didn't want to be a disappointment to her husband, so he would have to practice this position with her until she got it perfect. She would need to learn to enjoy it completely and eagerly welcome it so she could satisfy her husband completely. It would require them to practice this position for hours each day so she could perform it flawlessly.

He had told her not to worry. He was sure by the time the baby was born, she would be so good at it, it would be as natural as breathing to her. It would also prevent future pregnancies which her husband would expect her to be responsible for. He would not stand for her being pregnant more than a few times. Husbands wanted thin, pretty wife's who were eager to please them. Not beaten down blimps who were disgusting to look at and revolting to have sex with.

She was so happy papa had given her to such a loving and caring "father" who would look after her and teach her all the things she needed to know to be a good wife. He never tired of showing her all the things she needed to learn and spent all his free time alone with her. He even called her his "little pet" and let her sleep with him every night. Afraid the other children would become jealous because she was his favorite and try to harm her. They were never given the special little treats she was and he made no secrets about it to his children. He told them she was his "special little pet" and they were to treat her so. Pampering her just as he would. If he heard anything different from her, they would answer to him and the consequences would be severe.

She reassured her brothers there was nothing to worry about. She was in very loving hands. He treated her better than any daughter could have hoped for and would treat their baby just as kind. He had even promised her, she could live with him until he found the perfect husband for her. But there was no hurry for that, he'd said. He enjoyed sharing himself with her each day. Helping her practice all the things he'd worked so hard to teach her. He knew she enjoyed sharing herself with him too, by how eager she was to please him.

When the time was right he would pick out a few men he felt would make her a good husband. She would stay with each of them for a few months or more. Sharing herself with them, as she did with him. She would be expected to do everything a good wife would do and much more, because it would be up to them to decide if they wanted to keep her or not. She had assured him, with adoring eyes, that when the time came she would do everything necessary to make him proud of her. He had smiled at her and gently held her as he kissed her deeply, searching her mouth with his tongue, until she began to melt like hot butter in his hands. Then he turned her gently around, firmly grabbing her arms as he did and plunged himself deep and hard into her backside. Continuing to plunge deeper and harder each time he did, until he had completely ravished her bottom.

She had screamed out in such agony, he had covered her month with his hand and told her to relax and trust him. He was only showing her what her husband would expect her to do for him once they were married and he wanted her to be prepared. He was only trying to protect his "little angel" by showing her why he didn't want to marry her off right now, to a husband who would play too rough with her.

She was "Daddy's" special "little girl" and he would keep his "little girl" right beside him until he felt the time was right for her to become a wife, if that time ever came. But "Daddy" was in no hurry to marry off his "little girl". She was his perfect "little pet" and the only way he could be sure she was treated right, was to keep her to himself. He would continue to share her lessons with her, including the one they had just shared together, so she would be ready when the right husband came along. But for now "Daddy" wanted his "little girl" all to himself, where he could keep her safe and show her how much he loved and needed her.

And if he never found the prefect husband for his "special little pet", Daddy would let her stay with him forever. Becoming both her "husband" and "Daddy". Then they could play only the husband games, the ones she knew were "Daddy's" favorite. (He had gotten so excited thinking of playing husband games with her for a life time, he had wanted to take her again right there.)

Tears welded up in her eyes as she told her brothers this. Saying she loved "Daddy" so much, she never wanted him to find her a husband. That way she could stay with him forever as his "little girl" and wife.

Her brothers had heard more than enough. They were beyond enraged. They were teetering on the brink of berserk. How dare that bastard use their little sister like that. Anyone who had ever seen her knew she was simple. Unable to understand how wrong the things he was doing to her were. They would make him pay for what he'd done to her. Losing all sense of reason, they burst through the door of the house and grabbed him by the neck. Then took turns beating him to death with their fists.

When they were done, they dragged him to the woods out behind the house and buried him. They knew no one would be coming after them or questioning how he died. This was considered backwoods justice. Once the truth was known, they would only be sorry they hadn't killed him themselves. They would now have to take their sister home, heavy with child, to a family already struggling to survive. It was almost too much to cope with. But they had managed before and they would just have to figure out a way to manage again.

CHAPTER 9

Edward's mother couldn't have been happier knowing her father was dead. He was the most evil and vile person she had ever known. He managed to contaminate and destroy everything he touched and no one was safe from him. She was sure there would be no one who missed him. He had, had mistresses every year since the day he and Mama had married and managed to keep them all constantly pregnant. You would have thought he was trying to populate the entire world all by himself. But he had no shame about him. He wanted what he wanted and would destroy anyone who got in his way.

At first he had tried to at least keep his mistresses a secret. But after a while he decided it was just easier for him to keep them all under one roof. He had tried to convince Mama at first that he was just helping out a poor little girl who had been taken advantage of and misused by her brothers. But after the poor little girl gave birth and continued to have baby after baby in secession, she knew the babies could only be Papa's. He had moved her out of their bedroom when he first brought the little girl home. Saying as young as she was, he would need to keep a close eye on her and this was the easiest solution for everyone. He had certainly kept a close eye on her as he filled her belly with one baby after another.

By this time Papa had lost all interest in Mama, but thought it was important to continue to keep her pregnant. That way she would have no other choice but to stay with him and keep their secret safe. Women were often very sensitive about other women, especially the ones their husbands kept as mistresses and he didn't want her to get any ideas about causing trouble for him. He rarely spent time with her anymore, unless he was trying to get her pregnant again. Then he would stop at nothing to convince her how much he really loved her and wanted to share that I love by having another baby with her. He would really turn on the charm. Kissing her tenderly and deeply, giving her his undivided attention. Making love with her as often as he did with his mistresses. Even moving from his mistress bed to hers in order to further convince her it was only her that he loved.

He had told her she was the only woman he had ever loved and the others were nothing more than distractions for him. Sexual objects he could relieve himself with, to ease the burden on her and nothing more. Making it even more believable by talking harshly to his mistress and demanding that she take complete responsibility for the care of his beloved wife. She was in on the plan to deceive his wife, so she didn't take offence to his orders. It was as much in her best interest to keep the wife out of the way as it was his. They both should have been on a stage some where, as cleverly as they had managed to deceive her.

The mistress had been ordered to go to her own closet and pick out the two prettiest dresses she had, then get her two sexiest nighties and bring them all back and give them to his wife. When she returned with the items he had requested, he ordered her to draw a bath for his wife and bathe her. Then dress her in the pretty under garments he had just bought her and one of the dresses she had given her. She took very special care with his wife. Bathing her till her body and hair glistened and then arranging her hair in a very becoming style. Massaging warm oil all over her body just before she dressed her. After she had completed this routine with her, he would take his wife into town and wine and dine her. Letting her choose anything from the menu she desired. Urging her to splurge on herself and order the expensive dessert for herself too.

After a month of such extravagant treatment for her, she would again be pregnant and he could end the game. Going back to sleeping with his mistress and showering her with all the attention he had just given his wife. His wife would be devastated and crying. Begging him not to leave her again and destroy the love they had once again found together, But by this time he was done with her and barely knew she was alive. He would show her very little attention until the baby was born and then he would start the cycle all over again. Begging her to forgive him and asking to be welcomed back into her loving arms. Telling her what a terrible mistake he had made in letting her go. But if she gave him another chance he would never leave her again. Of course he didn't mean a word he said and as soon as she was again pregnant he would avoid her like the plague.

This went on for years. His game getting more detailed and elaborate as the years past. She would always take him back. Hoping this time he would really keep his promise to her. But of course he never did. After his current girlfriend had managed to have four babies with him in less than four years. She called it quits. His girlfriends were getting younger and younger each year and having babies with him at an alarming rate. She couldn't complete with these girls any longer, if she ever could. Many of them were younger than her older daughters. She realized then that she had never been anything more than a baby factory and housekeeper to him.

It broke her heart, that even with all he had done to her, she still loved him. He treated her worse than trash, but at least he still knew she was alive. She was so in love with him she would have done anything he asked. She knew he was only using her, but she seemed powerless to stop him. As long as she lived, he would continue to heap unspeakable abuse on her and she would gladly welcome it just to be near him. Even as she heard herself say these things, she couldn't help thinking how desperate and pathetic she sounded. She knew only in death would her pain be eased. He would eventually kill her with his abuse and God save her she would loving let him. Never raising a hand to stop him. But weeks later she did stop him. Finally finding the courage to end her life and stop the pain she had endured from him for years.

He cared so little about her, she was barely cold in the ground before he brought in her replacement. A 13 year old "housekeeper" who was suppose to help around the house. But didn't seem to be doing any work around the house, other than for Papa. Like all his other "housekeepers" she had been sleeping in his bed since the day she had gotten there and took orders only from Papa. After three months of her being there, her belly began to expand considerably and looked like she had swallowed a basketball. Telling them what they already knew. She was Papa's new lover.

She was actually a bit older than Papa liked his lovers. But she was rather slow and it made her appear to be much younger than she was. Papa seemed obsessed with her and made it clear to them that she was the "Queen" of the house. Anything she sked, no matter how small, was to be done for her immediately. The thoughts of having to deal with another one of Papa's little girls turned her stomach. But she knew Papa had far worse ghosts in his closet than his.

Her three older sisters had, had to marry men more than twice their age, because of Papa's nightly visits to their rooms. Visits he had continued with her younger sisters, once they were gone. Even with all the women Papa brought home, the nightly visits to her sisters rooms had never stopped or even slowed down. He planned on finding them husbands too, once his evil pleasures began to swell in they bellies and become evident to the world. He would never allow himself to be discovered for who he was and would do anything to keep it from happening.

She had been spared this humiliating shame because she had looked too much like Mama. Papa had visited her once when she was very young and told her he would never "tuck" her in like he did her sisters. She looked too much like her mother and the thoughts of sliding under the covers to share a bed with her, made him sick. He was sure no other man would ever want to share a bed with her either. But now that Papa was dead, they could all breathe a sigh of relieve. Their "house of horrors" was finally over and they would never have to worry about being fondled and violated by him again.

All that was left for the family to do now, was to find families for all the siblings. Her two brothers had taken on that task themselves and given her the job of cleaning out Papa's room. It turned out to be quite an easy job for her, because she threw out everything that was his. But when she started to clean out the closet, she ran across a pile of legal stuff and decided to put it in the box that was already in the closet. What a surprise she got when she took off the lid and found it filled with money. She didn't stop to count it, but she was sure it was more money than she had ever seen. Suddenly she was enraged and wished she could have killed him herself.

She couldn't remember a day that her family hadn't been on the brink of starvation. Wearing old clothes that their neighbors had thrown out and wondering how long it would be before their next meal. All the while her father was sitting on a gold mine that could have fed and clothed them for years. Just another example of how truly selfish he was. Never caring that his wife and children were starving, as long as he could continue to live the good life.

It was her brothers who had finally found jobs to support the family, which was no small task. They had somehow been able to find jobs that paid well enough for them to buy food on a regular basis, pay rent and still have a little left over. Which her brothers would normally spend on clothes and shoes that were desperately needed by the whole family. They were starting to look like normal people again. Not the herd of vagabonds they had looked like before. They had no idea what kind of job their brothers had, but after a lifetime of struggling just to survive they didn't really care.

At least they didn't think they cared. But if they had known that robbery was how they got their money, they may have changed their minds. The brothers hadn't really wanted to do robberies, but they knew no ordinary job could provide the amount of money they would need to take care of such a large family. So the two brothers had resorted to robbery.

They would go to the local tavern each night, along with most of the men in town. Grab a couple of beers they made last all night and head to the back room where the men were playing cards. They would watch the men play all night. Careful to see who the big winners were. Then just before closing they would leave the tavern. Walk to the alley near by and wait for the winners to leave the tavern too. Winners who were now barely able to walk after their night of drinking. They were just ripe for the picking. When they saw them near the alley, they would befriend them and lead them away from the crowd. Directly into the alley where they would proceed to rob them. Taking all the money they had just won and anything else they might be able to pawn.

They would quickly head home after the robberies and store the money in their closet, under its fake floor. Making sure that even if the sheriff came to search their home, they were unlikely to discover the money. They had been doing this for quite some time now with no problems. But they knew it was only a matter of time before someone discovered it was them. They had wanted to get out of town before that time came, but couldn't bring themselves to leave the family to fend for itself. But with Papa dead their problem were now solved.

They had found homes for all of their siblings including Edward's mother, but she refused to go. Saying she was old enough now to take care of herself. But that was just a little too vague for the brothers. After a lengthy discussion between the three of them, they agreed that living up North with one of her sisters would be acceptable. Now they would just need to find out if any of the sisters were willing to take her.

Within days they received word, that indeed, one of her sisters would be thrilled to have her. Edward's mother was thrilled as well and offered to pay her own way. But her brothers refused to let her. Saying that this may be the last time they ever saw each other and they wanted to do this for her before they left. She reminded them of the money she had found in Papa's closet, but they told her to keep it. She would need it a lot more than they would.

The next day they all headed down to the train station and her brothers bought her a one way ticket to her sister's. Before she got on the train, they hugged and kissed goodbye one last time. The brothers could feel her tremble as they held her and the tears in her eyes as she got on the train. They knew she was scared, but they also knew she would be alright. She was a fighter and had survived worse things than this in her short life. They only hoped she would be able to find joy and happiness where she was going. Something she had been denied so far.

Now with everything settled, it was time for them to decide what to do with their lives. They certainly couldn't stay here unless they planned on spending the rest of their lives in jail, but they really didn't have anywhere to go. With no options available, they decided that joining the Army would probably be their best bet. With most of Europe already at war and the United States pledging their support, it would only be a matter of time before they were drafted anyway. They would both go to the recruiting office tomorrow and begin their lives anew. Their family was all gone now and would never be again. It was time for them to move on and start again, just as the others had already done.

CHAPTER 10

Edward's mother's new life was beginning to shape up rather nicely. Her sister and brother-in law had welcomed her with open arms. Refusing the money she had offered them for her room and board, saying they wouldn't hear of it. They were just grateful they had an opportunity to take her in and make her a part of their family. Her brother-in law knew how much his wife missed her family, except her father of course, and was happy she was reunited with her.

Edward's mother couldn't believe how lucky her sister was to be married to a man as kind as her husband. The marriage may have been forced on her because of the situation her father had put her in. But her sister couldn't have been more blessed if she had picked him out herself. Edward's mother would go on to live with them for several more years, until the man she would marry walked off a boat from the war in Europe.

He had spent the last two years in Europe and returned a decorated hero. His duty to his country was now paid and he could resume his life. He had moved in with his parents just long enough to get settled. As soon as he got a job and put some money aside he would move to a place of his own. But while he was there he had noticed the pretty young lady that lived two doors down from his parents house and decided he wasn't in as big a hurry to move as he thought.

It had been hard at first landing a job with all the veterans now returning home and needing jobs themselves. But within the month he was finally hired at the only factory in the area. Much to his surprise the pretty young girl down the street also worked there. She wasn't one of the factory workers, but the girl in charge of the lunch cart. She would set her cart up inside the break room during lunch and sell sandwiches and coffee to the workers. She had been hired by a local Deli who provided the cart and fresh sandwiches each day to sell inside the factory. The food and coffee was so good that it normally sold out before the lunch hour was over.

It didn't take him long to decide that he would buy his food at work, instead of bringing it from home. He quickly introduced himself to the young lady, but she seemed mistrusting and guarded towards him. That was probably only natural though, being she was the only women in a factory full of single men. But he wasn't one to give up easy. No to him only meant he needed to try harder. He was by no means the best looking guy in the factory, but he was definitely the most persistent.

His hard work finally paid off and she agreed to have dinner with him one night after work. After only a few dates they both knew that they were meant to be together for a life time. They knew life was short and didn't see any reason not to marry immediately. Within the week they had gone to the Justice of the Peace and become husband and wife. Renting a tiny little apartment within walking distance of his parents and her sister.

As they settled down and began their life together, they knew they were a match made in Heaven. He was a good worker and an excellent provider for the two of them. They were so in love and had a passion between them that would never burn out. People who knew them, predicted this was one marriage that would last forever and there was no reason to believe it wouldn't.

But as the first year of marriage ended there were signs that something was wrong. They were still very much in love, but the horrors of war he had seen were beginning to take a toil on him. He had tried to deny there was anything seriously wrong, but she knew differently. There was no denying the blood curdling screams at night and the uncontrollable sobbing as he slept. The horrors of war would give him no peace and many nights he would wake up soaked in his own sweat and shaking. The dreams were so real, he was sure he was still in Europe, fighting a war that had taken so many lives and destroyed so many families. When he awoke in the morning he would try to act as though nothing had happened.

Alcohol would ease his pain for a while, but the horrors of war would always return. Hiding just around the corner, waiting to pounce on him again. As the nightmares continued, he began drinking more and more to block them out. But no matter how much he drank, he couldn't stop the nightmares for long. He knew he was fighting a losing battle, but for now it was all he had.

By the end of their second year of marriage they were expecting their first baby. He couldn't have been more pleased or proud and when the baby finally arrived and was a boy, he couldn't have asked for more. He was the father of a healthy baby boy and he would try to be the best father any child could want. He spent all his free time with his wife and baby son. There wasn't anything he wouldn't do for the two of them. They were his whole life.

He continued to fight the demons in his head and put the war behind him. But as time went on the demons only got worse. He had continued to drink to forget the war, but it was now interfering with his home life. Namely his wife and son. He was determined that nothing would interfere with them and gave up drinking for good. But this had only intensified his nightmares and was beginning to affect every area of this life. It was at this time he decided to silence the demons for good. He would not let the demons destroy his family too. They were the best thing in life he'd ever known and he would thank God in Heaven for them when he arrived.

Sometime in the night his wife was awaken by the sound of a loud boom. It sounded to her like a gun firing, so she got up to investigate. When she turned on the light she saw her husband laying on the floor with blood seeping out of a bullet wound to his head. She called for help immediately, but knew it was already too late. When he was pronounced dead her whole world came crashing down. Besides her son, he had been the only thing in life that had truly loved her and now he was gone.

She had walked through the following week in a daze. Numb from the incredible pain she felt. This must have been the way her husband felt for the last seven years. Towards the end she could see and feel the pain he was going through. But she had no way to help him and she could tell he knew it too. She wished there had been some other way to end his pain, but she knew there couldn't have been or he would never have left them.

Through it all she had felt his love for her and their baby boy. That love had been so strong and now their little boy of five would never know that love or remember what a wonderful father and husband they had been blessed with. They were all alone in the world now and all they had left of him was the beautiful memories he had given them. She had left the picture of him, in his army uniform, still on the mantle. For all the pain the war had caused him, he had still been so proud of how bravely he had fought for his country. There wasn't a day that went by, he didn't stop to look at the picture and gently lay his hand across it. The war had taken his life, but the picture would remain of the man, few men are brave enough to become.

She was sure her heart would never mend or stop missing the man she loved so much. Wishing daily he was still with her. But he would have wanted her to go on. To raise their little boy the way he would have raised him if he were still alive. That was the least she could do for the wonderful man who had shown her what it was to be loved and how to love in return.

She knew she needed to get on with her life. It had been weeks since she buried her husband and the little money they had saved would soon be gone. She would have liked to stay in the tiny apartment they had always called home. But the memories here were still too fresh and continually reminded her of how much she had lost. She knew she needed to move somewhere new and leave the past behind.

Her life and son's needed to move forward. Continuing on a new path that would honor the memory of her husband.

Honor the way he had taught her to be brave by the way he had lived. She would do all she could to make him proud of her. Proud of how hard she worked to provide a good home for their son.

She eventually decided to move back in with her sister. Deep inside she was scared and lonely and didn't know what to do. But on the outside she tried to look brave for the sake of her son. Her husband had always taken care of things in the past and she had let him. But he was gone now and she would have to make the decisions herself. Deciding how they would live and how to go about making it happen. She felt so overwhelmed right now she wasn't sure she could. But her sister would soon help her find the way.

Her sister and husband had noticed how lost and struggling she was and invited her to come live with them. They had loved having her live with them before she had married and this would give them the chance to be a support system for her. Helping her manage the rocky road ahead. She was so relieved to have someone to help her, all she could do was hug her as tears of joy ran down her face. She loved her so much at this moment she never wanted to let her go, but knew she must. Managing to compose herself, she finally let go. Thanking her again and again for offering their home to her and her son.

As soon as she was moved in, her sister began taking care of them as though they were guests. Doing everything for them and asking nothing in return. As much as she enjoyed the way her sister was taking care of her she felt guilty at the same time. She tried in small ways to show her how much she appreciated her, but she knew it would take a lifetime to repay her kindness.

She was finally working now. Two jobs in fact and would soon be able to pay her share. Not that her sister was asking, but she wouldn't have it any other way. Her sister and husband had been so generous to her, both emotionally and financially, she wanted to pay them back in any way she could.

Working two jobs had really been hard on her and her son. It left very little time for them to be together. But once again her sister had come through and offered to babysit him while she was at work. Her husband made enough money she didn't need to work. She was a full time housewife with kids of her own to raise. "One more would be no trouble", she had said. Her son would have his cousins to play with and an aunt who loved him. This really put her mind at ease and once again she had no words adequate to thank her. She could work now with peace of mind. Not worrying whether her son was being well taken care of or not.

But the grind of her two jobs began to take a toil on both of them. She was so busy working she hardly had time to see him. She felt more like a distant relative than his mother. It broke her heart she couldn't see him more, but nothing could be done. They needed the money and just one job would not provide enough. She was doing the best she could and she knew once her son was grown he would realize it too.

But the years took a terrible toll on both of them. Causing his mother to look far older than she was and her son to never know a mother's love. His aunt was good to him and his cousins, but it wasn't the same as being loved by a mother. And as good as his aunt tried to be, she basically left them to raise themselves. Spending her days on the couch, drinking, smoking and watching television. She would order lunch out and give them money enough to pay the delivery boy when he arrived. They would eat their lunch at the table by themselves and then go out to play. When school was in session she didn't even need to do this. She would send them to school with lunch money and they would eat in the lunch room with the rest of the kids.

She never needed to cook for herself because she was never hungry. With all the drinking and smoking she did she never had an appetite. She spent all her days the same way. Drinking, smoking and watching television. The only time she left the house during the day was when she needed to buy more alcohol or cigarettes. But lucky for the children it never seemed to effect her mood. She was always sweet and fun loving no matter how much she had drank.

The only other time she managed to move off the couch was each day right before her husband got home. Then she would jump up from the couch and go through the house like a whirlwind. Picking things up and putting them away so it looked like she had been working all day. Shouting orders at the kids to quick help her so they could get as much done as possible. But even this was done good heartedly. She made sure on Saturday's that each of them had enough money to go to the movies and buy refreshments too. It was her way of thanking them for all their help.

All in all Edward's childhood was pretty good even if it was a little neglectful and short on a mother's love. He had classmates he knew that were far worse off than him. But he would soon find out that growing up in such a chaotic household would bring him untold problems in adulthood. Especially in marriage.

CHAPTER 11

With all the excess baggage they would both bring to the marriage, it was only natural there would be problems. But she had no idea the enormity of those problems. It began as a marriage made in Heaven. But it wouldn't be long before she would see the real Edward. An Edward she never knew existed. This Edward looked very much like someone else she knew and the feeling was unnerving.

The more she was around Edward, the more she felt like she was living with her mother all over again. Not so much in a physically abusive way, but more in an emotional abusive way. It began very subtle at first. His way of helping her. But it became clear very shortly that he was anything but helpful.

She refused to believe it was true at first. He had been so kind and caring while they were dating. He had shown her in endless ways how much he loved and cared for her. She couldn't believe he was really the person she was seeing. She felt no one could be that good of an actor. But she would soon realize that she had severely underestimated him. She would come to see first hand how ruthless and cunning a human being can be. Defending his actions in the name of love.

She couldn't understand how he could have learned to be so ruthless and cunning. Nothing of what she had been told of his childhood would explain it. From what he had told her his childhood seemed pretty normal. Sure the death of his father was tragic! But even that was somewhat normal for the times. He had told her his father died when he was very young, not that he had committed suicide. Though in all fairness maybe he hadn't been told either.

He seemed rather well adjusted at times, but then he would do the most selfish and irresponsible things imaginable. She felt being raised full time by his aunt and among his cousins, he should have been better adjusted than that. But here again she had no idea he and his cousins had raised themselves.

He had only talked in glowing terms about his aunt. Not about the neglect. If she had known this it would have made understanding him easier. Not that she would have liked his behavior any better. But at least she would have understood where it was coming from. Based on what she knew, he just appeared to be a spoiled brat who cared only for himself. He wanted what he wanted and that was that.

She gently tried to help him understand how damaging his behavior was. How used and abused she felt when he spent all his nights out partying with his friends until all hours of the morning. How much she and the children needed him at home and how much they missed him when he was gone. But he worked full time and thought that was all he owed the family.

In time she would realize this was mild compared to what he was capable of. And his escalating bad behavior would contribute to an unresolved war between them that she wouldn't have wished on anyone. The promise of a marriage made in Heaven was quickly turning into a nightmare. But she wasn't a quitter and finally realized if she was going to have a life worth living she would have to carve it out for herself and children.

It was really quite sad. When they had, had their first child he had seemed happy. He was a wonderful father and would spend evenings playing with the baby. Reading her simple little bedtime stories and tucking her in at night. As more children came he seemed to be just as loving and caring as he had always been. As they became older there would be trips to the zoo and picnics in the park as a family. There were even visits to his aunt's house where his mother still lived.

But gradually things began to change. It was almost as though the children had been like a new toy to him. He had played with the new "toys" while they were still new, but now they were growing old and weren't fun anymore. He began to spend less and less time with the children, until he wasn't spending any time at all with them. It had been so long since he had read to the children at night, she wasn't sure the children even remembered he ever had.

He now seemed preoccupied when he was home. Always yelling at the children for the least little thing they did. Any time or money she spent on them would irritate him further. It was almost as though he had grown to hate them. The children he had once spent so much time with he now resented because of the demands they put on this time and money. He was forever coming up with reasons why he wouldn't be home in the evening. He was becoming more of a visitor to the house than a husband and father.

The ironic thing about this was that it was him who had insisted on having children. When she and him had first married she knew it was a marriage that was only seen in fairy tales. She was so glad she had married him. He made life so much easier. To be loved and cared for made you believe anything in life was possible. She felt this was as good as it got and couldn't have wished for anything more. But Edward thought otherwise. He thought children would be an expression of their love for one another and would only deepen the love they now felt for each other.

She hadn't been so sure. She loved children as much as he did. But she had seen the world out there and it wasn't a pretty sight. It was cold and cruel and she wasn't sure it was a world she wanted to bring children in to. But he convinced her that as loving and patient a person as she was, she would show them only the happiness in life. She had finally relented and realized after the birth of their child, it was one of the best decisions she had ever made. She was born to be a mother and thanked God every day for the gift he had given them.

She went on to be blessed yet again and then decided they had, had enough. She didn't want to be so worn out by a house full of children she couldn't enjoy the ones she had. She had also seen how scorned and ridiculed children from poor families were and she didn't want that for them either. She had children she deeply loved and would do anything for now, but also had a husband who detested the very children he had so desperately wanted. She had hoped things would improve, but that was only a dream too.

She had always tried to maintain her good looks and stay the same size she was when they had married. Even after giving birth to several children. She also managed to set aside time each week just for the two of them. Believing that a strong relationship between the two of them was the cornerstone of a solid family. It had to be solid so their relationship as parents would be solid too. But the fact that she seemed to handle all the demands on her time so well simply made Edward angrier and more distant.

The tension between them had grown so bad that one day he just exploded. "I love you Savannah, he said but I am sick to death of hearing about you from others. The noble Savannah who married Edward Brooks despite what people said. Savannah the perfect wife and mother. Still as pretty as the day she married. And did you know she even manages to make time to work with an Inter City Outreach program? I'm sick of it Savannah! Do you hear me! Sick of it!"

"Is it too much to ask that I be given a little credit once in a while? Would it be so hard for someone to say. "That Edward Brooks, such a kind and loving person. Such a good provider too. And hasn't he made something of himself, coming up the way he did? But no! It's just poor stupid Edward. Born on the wrong side of the tracks. Saved only by the grace of God and the beloved Savannah. It isn't fair Savannah. It isn't fair you got it all!"

Savannah felt tears forming in her eyes as Edward spoke. She reached out to touch him and let him know she felt his pain and cared. But Edward pulled away as though he had been touched by a hot iron and walked away.

All he'd ever wanted in life was to be admired and accepted. The funny thing was, Savannah was the only one who had ever done that. The only one who hadn't cared where he came from, only who he was. And she was the one person who would eventually destroy him. No matter how hard he tried, Savannah would always out shine him. Savannah was blessed by the Gods and there was very little she hadn't been given. His friends had been right about all they had said. That was really what had gotten to him.

She was a patient and loving mother whose children adored her. She had the voice of an Angel and athletic skills he could only dream of. She could cook and sew and fix almost anything that broke. He could barely hammer a nail straight! He was sure there must be something she couldn't do, but he hadn't found it yet.

He knew she loved him dearly, but he was nothing around her. He wasn't talented in any way, other than having street smarts, which most of the kids he grew up with also had. He couldn't even brag about his looks because they were average too. He was the apodeme of the word average. They could have wrote the words "Edward Brooks" next to the definition of average in the dictionary. It would have been bad enough being married to "Mr. Everything." But a man being married to "Mrs. Everything" was impossible.

He was beginning to hate her. He knew he wasn't being fair, but he couldn't seem to stop himself. Most men would have felt blessed to have a wife like her. But she was taking a terrible toll on his ego. He would pick fights with her knowing none of what he said was true. But she could only see the good in people and would break down in tears when he attacked her. Not because she feared him, but because she couldn't understand where he could have gotten such ideas.

She was always willing to try harder so these misunderstandings wouldn't occur. But he was determined that trying harder would never be good enough. He knew he had no right to torture and belittle her. But somehow making her feel worthless and insecure made him feel better. If he could make her feel bad enough he might finally get a chance to shine.

Savannah couldn't understand what had happened to Edward. Living with him had become a nightmare. He had always been a loving and caring man. But no more. Lately her and the children couldn't seem to do anything right. He was forever criticizing and screaming at them for imagined infractions. They would end up going to bed at night in tears.

No matter what she cooked at night it wasn't right. Her clothing was always wrong and he thought her hair looked like Hell! He was constantly mad at the children and no matter how well she cleaned the house he would complain. The tension in the house was becoming unbearable. She didn't think the situation could get much worse, but it did.

Edward who had always prided himself on being a good provider began neglecting the bills. Several times he had even refused to give her money for groceries. He had decided she no longer needed to drive the family car and removed the battery so it wouldn't run. His nasty remarks and constant criticism was also taking their toll. She would never have believed that something that had started so wonderful could have become so ugly. She had tried to be patient with him hoping things would improve. But it seemed the nicer she was, the meaner he became.

He had allowed the house to become so run down, she was afraid it would be condemned. The children were beginning to outgrow all their clothes, but he refused to give her any money to buy new ones. Even though he continued to spend a fortune on himself. The only way she had of getting around was the elderly man next door. He had told her he enjoyed her company and would be happy to take her along whenever he went to town. So twice a week or so they would ride in town together and she would get what she needed.

She knew he didn't need her company, but was only being kind without embarrassing her but he was always great company. He knew she didn't have any way to get around and felt sorry for her and the kids, and by the time they usually got home from their adventures with him everyone was smiling and laughing. But on one such occasion the laughter died the minute she walked through the door. Because of Edwards neglect part of the leaking ceiling in the livingroom had collapsed on the floor. She could only thank God they hadn't been home at the time or they may all have been injured or killed.

She couldn't believe she had let this situation go on for so long. Because she had refused to stop Edward in the past she had almost lost her children today. But no more! She had finally had enough. No matter what she had to do, the abuse was going to stop and stop now! She would rather die fighting than continue to live in this hell hole Edward had created. She didn't know what she was going to do. But she knew she was going to do something.

As she stood looking at the mess on the floor, Edward walked through the door. He noticed the mess too and looked up at her. Driven by absolute rage she yelled - spit the words at him as she spoke. "Because of your neglect of this house and the people who live here, we were almost killed today. You treat us little better than animals. But no more! I have had enough. I was the one person in your life who always treated you as an equal. I never judged you for your past, but only for who you were and this is the way you treat me? Well your reign of terror is over. We won't live like this another day. I will stop you or go to my grave trying."

Before she could raise her hand to block it, Edward slapped her with a stinging blow. "Don't you ever forget I'm the boss around here and I'll do as I please, he said. If you ever raise your voice to me again you'll get more of the same." As he turned to walk away she clearly understood the meaning of "Desperate people are the least intimidated." His blow had done nothing but reinforce her determination to stop him. She couldn't let him scare her now. She had too much to lose. She would stop him as she said she would and nothing or no one would get in her way. This was war and she had every intention of winning.

The force of the blow had brought tears to her eyes, but she would never let him see her pain. He would think the tears were from being struck by him. That he had broken her heart with his abuse. But their relationship had gone far beyond that. There was little he could do to her now that would surprise her or make her feel any more hatred toward him than she already did. It was time she taught him a lesson he wouldn't soon forget.

When she was reasonably sure he was asleep for the night she walked into the kitchen. She removed the butcher knife from the drawer and slowly walked to the bedroom where he slept. She quietly opened the door and entered without making a sound. As she neared the bed she covered his mouth with her hand and held the knife to his throat. In a chilling voice she spoke into his ear. "I believe every man is entitled to one mistake, but hear me now. My children and I will not live in a house of violence. If you ever raise your hand to me or mine again, I will slit your throat with a vengeance few men have ever witnessed. My father's Cheyenne blood runs deep and true through my veins and Cheyenne show mercy to no man they call an enemy, which you will surely be." With that said she removed the knife from his throat and slowly walked away.

She felt calmer and braver than she had felt in a very long time and it felt good. She knew she had to take a stand. She couldn't continue to live in fear and she didn't have the money to walk away. If a fight was what he wanted she'd give him one and she'd make a worthy opponent. She would have preferred to be loving and gentle in life. But she knew that wasn't possible with him. She had already tried that and it had almost cost her, her life and that of her children. She had been passive far too long and it was stopping now. They deserved better than this and she was determined to get it.

She would have to learn to be every bit as ruthless as he was, which she knew would be hard for her to do. But it had to be done. Her self esteem had reached an all time low and her self respect was all but gone. If she didn't confront him now and win she was afraid she never would. She would either teach him how to play nice with others and cooperate or she would make sure he didn't play at all.

Something had snapped in her today and she had found the fire and spirit she had once had. She had regained some of the inner strength that had brought her through so much of life's pain already. She planned on doing something with her life and God help anyone foolish enough to get in her way. God had once blessed her with so many gifts and talents. She only hoped if she dug deep enough she could still find them. She was certainly going to try.

CHAPTER 12

She got up the next morning while Edward was still asleep and took the battery out of his car to put into her own. Then took $50 out of his wallet and loaded the children into the car. They were going to the zoo today and have some fun for a change. They had been held prisoner in this house long enough. Starting today this was only one of many things that was going to change.

When she pulled into the driveway that night, Edward was waiting at the door. He looked ready to spit bullets. He told her he wanted the battery back and he wanted it back now! She told him she was sorry but they had plans for tomorrow. Maybe he could get his mother to help him or put the battery he had taken out of her car into his. He raised his hand as if to strike her and she said in a voice as cold as ice, "I hope you're not foolish enough to think I was bluffing last night Edward. I meant every word I said. Now if you'll excuse me, the children and I are hungry."

When she got up the next day she noticed Edward had found a battery for his car somewhere. She suspected it was the one he had taken out of her car a while back. Before he left for work she asked him if she could have some money to buy groceries. They had been out of milk for over a week and there was very little else to eat as well. Edward said he was sorry, but he didn't have any money. She knew he was lying because she had seen a wad of money in his wallet last night. But she smiled sweetly at him as she said, "That's alright Edward. I know you wouldn't let your children go hungry if you had the money. I'll just have to think of something else to do."

When Edward finally left for work she began to look around for something she could sell or pawn. She'd been telling the truth this morning when she had said there was little in the house to eat. She had thought of selling the television, but it was something the whole family enjoyed so much. She was hoping it wouldn't come to that. This whole thing made no sense anyway. Edward had a good job and made a great deal of money. But you would have never known it by looking at anyone but him. He made his family go hungry and his children walked around looking like rag muffins.

Just then she spotted Edward's golf clubs sitting in the corner. His new graphite golf clubs. How like Edward to have new clubs while his family went hungry. But then what would Edward know about being hungry? He made sure that he had something to eat whether his family did or not. She loaded the golf clubs and the children into the car and drove to the local golf shop. She knew they bought used clubs because Edward had made fun of the men who had bought them. She had no idea what the clubs were worth, but if the price sounded right she would accept it.

When she arrived and showed the clubs to the owner, he was very impressed. Stating that the clubs were in such good shape they looked new (which she knew they were). He

offered her $700 for them and told her he would be happy
to look at any other clubs she had as well. She didn't know
if the price he was offering her was good or not. But she did
know it would help her buy many of the things they urgently
needed. She decided to take the money and thanked him
as she left.

As they were leaving she breathed a sight of relief. It
was good knowing she had money to buy groceries and a
few of the many other things they needed. She would take
what was left of the money and hide it in the trunk of her
car under the spare tire. She knew this would be a safe place
because Edward had never changed a tire in his life and she
had no reason to believe he would start now.

Edward was rather late coming home that night. He had
spent most of the evening with his girlfriend. A girlfriend
he had worked very hard to keep a secret from her and the
family and the reason he never seemed to have enough
money. But she was too tired tonight to ask him where he
had been and was really not interested enough to care. God
only knew where he had been and she wasn't sure she wanted
to know anyway.

When Edward finally arrived home and seen the
children eating cookies he was rather surprised. He wondered
where Savannah had gotten the money. This morning he
had thought he would just let her go hungry a while. If
she got hungry enough she would come crawling back to
him, begging to be forgiven. He decided he would ask the
children. But when he did, they jumped up and ran to their
mother. That was when he noticed the golf clubs weren't in
the corner.

He could have sworn he had put them there just the

other day. The food was temporarily forgotten as he walked into the kitchen. Surely Savannah would know what had happened to them. When he asked her she said she had noticed how upset he was this morning. She knew it had really bothered him that he didn't have any money to buy groceries for his children. That was when she had noticed the golf clubs and decided to sell them to get some money.

She heard him say, "You Bitch" under his breath. But she continued to smile as she silently chuckled to herself. "That was a very loving gesture on your part Edward. Giving up your golf clubs for the children and me. We really appreciate it." She turned her most loving smile to her children. "We really should say thank you to your father children." The children responded in unison. "Thank you father". She then told the children to run along to their room and she would be in shortly to get them ready for bed.

When she heard them shut the door to their room she turned to Edward and nearly slapped him with her words. "You will either cooperate with this family or you and I are going to play hardball. And I warn you now, I plan on winning every confrontation we have. Living with you has made me as calloused and ruthless as you are. From now on you will give me the money I need each week to run this house or I will take matters into my own hands. It would be a shame to have to sell more of your expensive toys. But believe me I won't hesitate for a minute to do it". As she turned to leave Edward asked her how much she had gotten for the clubs. She half turned as she replied, "Not near what I needed" and left the room.

This was only the beginning of what Edward was in store for. It had been a long time since she had held him accountable for anything, least of all his family. But Edward would soon realize she meant business and she wasn't backing down. She may not have much money now, but she was going to change all that. She had found a new confidence and drive that would change her life for the better. She knew now the collapsed ceiling had been a gift from God. If it hadn't been for that, she wasn't sure how long she would have put up with this.

Edward would have loved to leave the family and let her figure out how to manage things on her own. But he couldn't have stood the criticism he would have gotten. Most thought he had the perfect wife and family. And he knew if the reason for the divorce got out he would be finished. Scorned by the very people who were now his friends.

He had liked it better when he was in charge and calling the shots. She had always been so sweet and patience he would never have thought she had this kind of fire in her. But he knew she meant business this time and he was beginning to worry. If she did find a way to get her life back on track and he didn't doubt she would, she may decide to divorce him. That would be just as bad as him leaving her because the facts of the divorce would still leak out. Which was exactly what he was trying to avoid.

He realized for the first time what he stood to lose if he didn't get his act together soon. He would need to play the perfect husband and father long enough to gain her trust back. Once she believed in him again he could gradually go back to his old ways. But for now he would need to heap loads of attention on her and the children to show them he was a changed man. This would be no easy task. He had done as he pleased for so long he wasn't sure he remembered how.

Sure he had charmed his girlfriend but that was different. She only needed a few nights alone with him each week and expensive gifts to be satisfied. But Savannah was different. She couldn't be bought. She wanted far more. His time, attention and involvement with the family. Something he really didn't want to give. But under the circumstances he didn't have any other choice. He would just have to let his girlfriend know what was going on and why they couldn't see each other for a while. At least until this all blew over and he had convinced Savannah he was a changed man. She wouldn't like it but there was nothing else to do.

He really enjoyed spending time with her, but she wasn't worth losing his family over. It would just take a little time before he could figure out how to have them both. Truth be told he actually enjoyed his girlfriend's company over Savannah's. She was a lot like him. Maybe a little more crude and rough around the edges. But she was his kind of people. He didn't have to put on "airs" around her or pretend to be anything he wasn't. They understood one another. Neither one of them being accepted by the "finer" people in life.

But this didn't seem to bother her as much as it did him. He had never understood this part of her. To him being accepted was everything. It was the only thing that really mattered. He had fought hard to rise above his raising and would do anything to stay there. He may prefer his girlfriend's company over his wife's but she could never give him the social acceptance he craved so much. Savannah was the only one who could do that. She could open doors for him he could never have opened for himself. His girlfriend knew this too and understood it. She didn't like it, but she understood it.

He may not have worried so much over her feelings though if he had known she had been plotting his wife's demise for quite some time. She had known that as long as his wife was around he would never leave her and if she left him he would do anything to get her back. There was no hope with her around that she would ever have him to herself. The thoughts of always competing against his wife with no hope of winning broke her heart.

His wife could have anyone she wanted, but Edward was the only one she had a shot at happiness with. She would always have to take what was left over in life and it just didn't seem right. Just once in her life she would have liked to be the "Bell of the Ball". Choosing who and what she wanted and having it returned to her in kind. But that wasn't likely to happen unless she did something to make it happen herself. Which was just what she was planned on doing.

Edward thought she didn't really care about social acceptance but she did. She cared just as much as he did. She just couldn't stand the pain of constantly being rejected. So she pretended not to care. Life just seemed easier that way.

CHAPTER 13

Edward was doing all he could to win back Savannah's love and trust. But it seemed the more effort he made in trying to please Savannah the less she cared. She had barely spoken to him since the night she had threaten to kill him. He couldn't say he blamed her. Up until now he hadn't given her much reason to care. He really wondered if he had waited too long this time. Finally burned one too many bridges to ever go back. He once had her heart for the taking. But he wasn't sure now if he could get it back at any price.

He didn't know why he had let his foolish pride and selfish ways ruin everything. She hadn't asked for much from him, but he had refused to give her even that. His presence now had no effect on her and the children refused to come near him. Every time he tried to interact with them they would run screaming to their Mother for protection. He had no idea how to win their trust back or begin to bond with them as a father.

He really hadn't cared until now and he only cared now because he was in so much trouble. He didn't know where to start and Savannah wasn't about to help him. She had seen him destroy them before with his empty promises and she wasn't about to help him do it again. He tried to convince her he had really changed this time, but she wasn't listening. She had heard this same story from him a million times before, with no results. She wasn't falling for it again.

He pleaded with her to believe him this time. But the only emotion he saw in her was the hatred that radiated from her eyes for him. A controlled rage she barely kept in check. He was working harder than he had ever worked in their marriage, but the look in her eyes told him it would never be enough. He had spent too many years pushing her away for her to care now. She wasn't letting her guard down around him for a minute.

He had tried everything to spend more time with the family, but she had refused. Claiming she was busy or the children weren't available. It didn't matter what he suggested to her it was never the right timing. He was sure she was doing this deliberately to make his life as miserable as possible and he couldn't say he didn't have it coming. He had dished it out for years and now he was getting a taste of his own medicine. She had spent years trying to get through to him, but he wasn't interested. Now that he was, she didn't care.

He knew if he didn't start making progress soon his life would all come crashing down. Between winning back his wife and keeping his girlfriend on hold, he wasn't sure how much more he could handle. His nerves were taking a beating and he was beginning to come unraveled. He knew he needed to be patient with himself and not give up, but this was a bit more challenging than he had expected. She had always been so sweet and patient, he couldn't believe she had this much fight in her. She was playing a lot harder this time than she ever had before.

But he still couldn't believe she would actually win. He had played this game too long and was convinced she was no match for him. He was sure it was only a mater of time before everything blew over and his life returned to normal. Big talk he knew, coming from him. He only hoped if he repeated it enough times to himself he would actually believe it. The stakes were so much higher this time, he knew he couldn't fail. The consequences were just to steep to consider.

But try as he might, he was getting no where with her. That is until he decided to start attending Church with her and the children. Up to this point they had always gone alone. He really didn't believe in the need to have God poking into his business every week. Pointing out all his shortcomings. The only time he really bothered with God was when he was in deep trouble. Then he would try anything he thought might help, including God. Which was the trouble he was in now.

It had proven to be the magic potion that turned everything around. If he hadn't been so self absorbed all those years he might have remembered how important religion was to her before now. Her whole face lit up that first Sunday they all went to Church together as a family. She was so proud to introduce him to her church family and have them welcome him with open arms. The minister had mentioned how pleased he was to see him there and hoped he would return again with his family.

He planned on returning alright until he had his family back in the palm of his hands. Then he would return to spending Sunday mornings the way he always did. In the bed of his girlfriend, getting all the blessings from her he could handle. Savannah would find herself once again attending Church alone. But he would be much more cleaver about it this time. So she would have no reason to suspect what he was really doing.

His weeks of Church attendance were working like a charm. He was beginning to melt the ice within her and could gradually see the hatred in her eyes for him slowly disappear. It wasn't long before he got her to agree to take the children with him to the zoo. It had taken some fast talking to finally convince her. But she had eventually agreed. It wasn't that she had finally begun to trust him again or anything. He wasn't that good of an actor. She was just hoping they could spend a nice day together for the sake of the children.

But even as she was agreeing to it, she had misgivings about it. She wondered if he really even meant it or was just playing games again. She didn't like to get the children's hopes up and then not follow through. But after talking to the children about the trip to the zoo with their father, she realized they didn't believe him either. Even at a young age they realized he couldn't be trusted. He had simply lied too often and broken too many promises for them to believe anything he said.

When Saturday came and Edward began loading the car for the zoo no one moved. They all expected this to be another one of his sick jokes. He was famous for loading them all into the car and then saying he had forgotten he didn't have any money. Or he would get their hopes up all week long and then announce Saturday morning that he had forgotten he had to work that day. She didn't believe he could ever undo all the damage he had done to them.

As they all stood there watching him load the car that day, they wondered what he would do next. Just then he yelled at them to hurry up and get into the car or they would be late. Savannah had been through this before too. Even if they did make it to the zoo, there was no guarantee they would make it in.

He had once taken them to the zoo and dropped them off at the gate. He said he would park the car and be right back. After an hour of waiting at the gate it had dawned on her he wasn't coming back. She'd had to use the money set aside for groceries to hire a taxi to take them home. He had made up some story about work he'd had to do at the office. He had said that as he was parking the car he realized he had forgotten to complete a report at work. He figured they could go through the zoo without him and he would pick them up later. It was only as he was driving home from work that night he realized he hadn't given them any money.

It was the most disgusting lie she had ever heard. She had eventually found a way to make him pay for what he had done. But she would never forget the humiliation and shame she had felt standing in front of the gate watching her children cry. Knowing their father had left them there and they wouldn't be able to see the zoo that day. But she was ready today. She had brought her own money and a credit card. No matter what he pulled today she was ready for him. And if this was his idea of another sick joke, it would be the last one he ever pulled on them.

All the way to the zoo she felt sick. She couldn't believe she had gone along with this. Her children trusted her so. She should have protected them better. She just knew Edward had something evil up his sleeve again. They had expected him to make up some excuse for not going again. But when he didn't, they seemed thrilled. It seemed they hadn't remembered the last time at the zoo as well as she had. Maybe standing in front of the gate for an hour hadn't been as traumatic for them as it had been for her.

When they arrived at the zoo she suggested Edward wait with the children this time while she parked the car. He gave her a rather dirty look, but didn't dare object. She only smiled at him in return. Once inside the zoo she couldn't believe what she was seeing. She was seeing an Edward she hadn't seen since they were first married.

He had bought them all lunch and ice cream cones. Then let them take as long as they wanted walking through the animal stations, feeding the animals as they went. Not complaining and sighing heavily as he normally would. Letting everyone know how put out and inconvenienced he was with the whole thing. She couldn't believe this was the same Edward who had made their last trip to the zoo a nightmare.

They had finished the day still laughing and happier than they could remember being as a family, in a very long time. No one said a single word on the way home that night. They were still soaking in the wonderful day they had just had and wishing it would go on forever. No one was more puzzled over the day they had just spent with Edward, than Savannah.

This was the man who had repeatedly tried to destroy them. He had done everything in his power to make their life as miserable as possible and now he was being nice? There was something very wrong with this picture and Savannah intended on finding out what. No one could spend that much time being evil, only to wake up nice one day. He was up to something and she was going to find out what. She didn't trust him any further than she could throw him. If he was being nice, there had to be a reason.

CHAPTER 14

Edward's nerves were at the breaking point. He was putting so much time and efort into winning his wife and children back, he was neglecting his girlfriend and she wasn't happy about it. He couldn't actually tell his girlfriend what he was really doing. She was still hoping he would leave Savannah and the girls and marry her. Between the sheets with her, he would promise her just about anything. But his real intention was to keep them both.

Lately to keep her happy he had been going into work early in order to take an extra long lunch hour. Then at lunch they would meet at his friends apartment and discuss their lives together between the sheets. His girlfriend was such an animal in bed he would have promised her anything. But lately the stress of his wife and girlfriend both, was getting to him. The constant attention they both demanded was wearing thin. He began sleeping with his newly hired secretary to release some of the additional stress.

He had hired her several weeks ago explaining that her duties would be of a more "personal" nature. When asked if she understood her job description, she stood up, walked around the desk and placed her hands in his lap. Gently rubbing him as she did. Smiling seductively as she unzipped his pants. He hired her on the spot. Spending the rest of the afternoon finalizing her "resume".

She was proving to be the best "secretary" he had ever hired. He was paying her twice as much as the other secretaries were getting and she was worth every penny of it. Generously rewarding him for all his effort and attention. Unlike his wife and girlfriend, who could be such "pains" most of the time, she was only too willing to do what he asked. Always throwing in just a little extra. She would come in early, stay late, and work weekends with him. Whatever he asked. He was sure the high salary and expensive gifts he gave her were a great motivator, but he was glad to pay her for what he wanted.

For some reason he needed this added excitement in his life to feel alive. A naughty little game he could play right under everyone's nose and get away with it. Who said he couldn't play by his own rules and win? Why he had to have a crisis brewing all the time just to feel alive he didn't know. He just knew he wanted to be the most important person alive. The center of the universe. To have praise heaped upon him. To be told how great he was and to NEVER, EVER be held accountable for anything he did.

Savannah was such a stuff shirt. Play by the rules! Take your punishment! Be responsible! But not him. He was different. Special. He didn't have to play by the same rules everyone else did. He would do what he wanted and escape the consequences. Or so he thought. His perfect little circus was about to come crashing down. And crashing down it did one Saturday night a few months later.

He was still juggling the girlfriend, the secretary, and the family, and feeling pretty smart about it. He had figured out how to have them all without any of them knowing about the other one. His finances were nearly in ruins, but other than that, he was still on pretty firm ground. He had no idea that tonight that ground would become shifting sand.

He had planned a nice evening out for the family. Pizza Play House for dinner, a movie, and Frosty Freeze for ice cream on the way home. He would be both Dad and Husband of the year after tonight. But after years of neglect and screw-ups, he needed to do something really great to win his family back. He had even invited his cousin and two nieces to go along, but they wanted to stay home and watch the beauty pageant on TV instead. Well actually stay home at his house instead. The pageant was on cable TV and they didn't have cable, but he did. Plus the temperature had been a sauna throughout the week. Well over a 100 every day. He had air conditioning but they didn't. He was more than happy to let them stay.

Since the incident with the collapsed ceiling, Savannah had begun making improvements to the house so he was no longer embarrassed to have people over. Even though he was the one responsible for the way it looked. Savannah had an eye for decorating and with the help of a handyman from her church, it was really beginning to look nice. He couldn't wait for his cousin and nieces to see it. They would be so surprised and happy for Savannah too.

His cousin knew how much Savannah liked that sort of stuff. They were close. Always had been. Even with all the tension between him and Savannah. In fact most who knew his cousin thought his wife and cousin were related, not him. His wife and cousin from a distance were often mistaken for the same person. Once up close, you could see the difference if you knew them well. But if not, it would have been very difficult. His wife was tall, slender, with green eyes and long blond hair. His cousin was the same height, weight and built, with blue eyes and just a slightly harder edge to her. And to make matters worse, the children had the same eerie likeness.

To those who knew them they could readily tell them apart, but to outsiders it was very difficult. His nieces were one year apart. The oldest had white/blond hair, blue eyes, very pretty, slim. The youngest had auburn hair, green eyes, average built, wore glasses. His oldest daughter had auburn hair, green eyes, average built and wore glasses. His second daughter was two years younger, but was tall for her age, had white/blond hair, green eyes, very pretty and very slim. As an outsider the cousin and two nieces looked exactly like the wife and two daughters. And if you were the angry girlfriend, there is no way you would have known the difference.

The evening began as normal as most. With Savannah, Edward and the girls leaving for a night of fun and his cousin and nieces settling in for a night of television and pizza. But the neighbors found something very strange about the pizza delivery boy that showed up an hour later with the delivery. On a day that had averaged 100, the delivery boy was wearing a windbreaker and baseball cap. Something the neighbors had noticed, because most of them were setting on their side porches trying to stay cool. Out of the sight of the delivery boy, but he was still within their sight. The boy was so slightly built, the jacket he was wearing almost looked too big for him.

As they watched the boy approach the house with the

order, what appeared to be Savannah and her daughters opened the door. As she did, the neighbors heard a secession of popping noises. Like the sound of an engine backfiring. As the popping noises continued, Savannah and her daughters fell to the ground. The delivery boy dropped the boxes and ran to his car. Speeding away like he was being chased.

The neighbors were horrified by what they had just witnessed and it took a few minutes for it to really register. When it did they sprain into action. Several calling the police and others going to Savannah and her daughters aid. When they arrived the doorway was covered in blood and the victims did not seem to be moving. The whole scene was surreal. Who could have done this? Who would have wanted to harm Savannah and her children? They were such good people and this was such a good neighborhood. How could this have happened?

As the neighbors waited for the police to arrive, they couldn't help but feel the pain of their loss. Someone had already felt for a pulse and realized there wasn't any. But as they looked closer at the victims they seemed to look different somehow. They looked like Savannah and her daughters, but they didn't. They weren't sure if the shock of what they had just witnessed was making their minds play tricks on them or not. Maybe being dead changed the way a person looked slightly. After all they had been shoot at such close range it was hard to really see them for all the blood. Who could have been so evil? Taking these little girls lives before they had barely begun? Denying them of such a good neighbor as Savannah. Hopefully, the police would soon be here to sort it all out and find the animal who had done this! This was a nightmare the neighbors would not soon forget.

CHAPTER 15

His girlfriend called from a payphone to say that she had done her part and now it was time for him to do his. Now that his wife and daughters were dead, there was nothing to stop them from getting married. He suddenly felt sick, realizing it hadn't been a home invasion after all. It had been his own girlfriend who had murdered his cousin and her girls. She couldn't even do that right! She had no idea she'd killed the wrong people. He couldn't figure out if she was a cold blooded murderer or just crazy.

As he was trying to decide, she interrupted his thoughts by saying she hoped he wasn't trying to back out of his part. Because things could get real ugly if he did. She wouldn't think twice about calling the police "Tip Line" and blaming it all on him. She would tell them he had hired a Hitman to kill his wife and kids for the insurance money. As for a motive, she would explain that he had a serious drug problem and owed a lot of money.

He was worried now, because she was just crazy enough to do it, and he did owe a lot of money. Not because he had a drug problem, but because he had too many women in his life. He needed to calm her down enough to convince her he was more than ready to do his part. That she was all he could think about day and night, and he had dreamed many times of the day his family would be gone so he could live the rest of his life with the only woman he ever loved. Hold her tight each night in his arms, as they made love long into the night, finally falling asleep exhausted in one another's arms. That the thoughts of having her all to himself, made him want to run right over and take her for himself now. But he knew they needed to wait a little while until everything died down. Otherwise, it might throw suspicion on them and then their perfect little life together would be ruined. He assured her they would marry the very minute it was safe.

She interrupted with the suggestion they fly to Vegas and get married in secret. Use one of those drive-thru Chapels. She had always dreamed of getting married in a huge church, filled with hundreds of people. With a rock size diamond ring and a custom made gown fit for a princess. But she would give up all those dreams to be his wife immediately. She loved him so much, there was nothing she wouldn't do to be his wife, as she had already proven. She was so happy he approved of what she had done and was as in love with her as she was him.

He nearly threw-up as he told her he loved her too and was counting the minutes until they could be together. She told him he could show her how appreciative he was on their wedding night. She giggled as she said "wedding night". He had to stay calm enough to get her off the phone and not give himself away. So he promised to sneak away tonight and show her a preview of what their "wedding night" would be like. So she would have something to hold on to until they were officially married. He would bring the wedding night "lace teddy" he had been saving for her. In the bright red, see-thru she had been begging for. Nothing was too good for the love of his life. He would make tonight so special, she may be disappointed on their wedding night. She assured him he could never disappoint her. He was the most wonderful man she had ever been with.

He wasn't sure how he could swing seeing her tonight, but he had to do something to stall for time. He had no intention of marrying her now or ever. Someone capable of murder was not the type of wife he had in mind. He would need to get his secretary to help him out of this jam. This was just the kind of situation she shined in. She was quite the actress and would give an award winning performance. She was meant to be on a stage somewhere. He had no doubts she would be eager to help him out with his little "problem" and he would gladly reward her. He would take her tonight with him and explain to his girlfriend that he had, had to bring her as part of his cover. No one would suspect anything if he was seen with his secretary. They often worked late together and were seen in each other's company all the time. (being lovers necessitated this.)

He would convince his girlfriend this was the only way they could see each other before the wedding. With his secretary in tow, he could make endless visits to her apartment and no one would be the wiser. He would gradually work the secretary into their sexual games, until he had convinced the girlfriend it was really her idea all along. By the time he was finished weaving his devious plan, his girlfriend would be as in love with his secretary as she was with him. Making it much harder for her to turn on either one of them.

If he ever did come under suspicion he would claim they

were both his girlfriends and he knew his secretary wouldn't hesitate to back him up. That would make the girlfriend look like a jealous lover, capable of murdering for the man she loved. He would be labeled an adulteress, but that was better than a murderer. If this was what he needed to do to make his girlfriend happy and stay out of jail, he'd do it!

When he talked to his secretary about helping him with his plan, she was only too happy to help out. She couldn't imagine someone doing something as terrible as his girlfriend had done and then blackmailing him over it. She was glad she could help him find justice in it all. He just needed to say the word and she would do it. What he couldn't know was why she had been so eager to help him. But it wouldn't be long before he found out she had an agenda of her own.

She had figured out that if he could afford to pay her as much money as he did, plus all the expensive extras, he could afford to keep her as his mistress too. To make sure he couldn't say no, she had stopped taking her birth control shortly after he had hired her. It was only a matter of time before she would be carrying his child. If the seed wasn't already planted inside her. Her family reproduced like rabbits, God love-em!, and she had no doubts she would conceive quickly too. They had managed to conceive quickly and arrange some pretty sweet deals from men because of it. They had taught her all she needed to know. Whether Edward agreed to keep her as his mistress or not, a child guaranteed he would be supporting them both for at least the next 18 years.

She was sure he would be furious once he realized she had used him too. But she would help him realize what a good plan this was for both of them. What a valuable asset she would be to him. Once he realized this, he would be hers for the taking. She would be the one he took to the office parties, on expensive business trips and out with his friends. Flaunting her as his arm candy, just to make them green with envy. And once the child was born she would make sure she looked better than she had, even before the child was conceived. She would look so good there would be no way he would ever let her go. She knew how to make herself indispensable and unlike his wife and girlfriend she wasn't looking for love or marriage.

What she was looking for was an endless supply of money and support (a sugar-daddy) and she would make it worth his time. She had a beautiful face and body and enjoyed sex as much as he did. Needed sex would have been more accurate. She craved it. Needed it as much as she needed the air she breathed. It was an all consuming compulsion for both of them. Always had been, even before they had met each other. They had both had more sexual partners than either one of them could count. That was probably why their first meeting had went so well. They had recognized that need in each other. That addiction that needed to be constantly feed. An addiction that was out of control.

She had to admit that the number of times they had been caught in the act would have embarrassed most people, but not them. Being bent over his desk, while he hammered her from behind or setting under his desk, giving him oral pleasure as he worked there only added to the excitement. Many a time she continued what she was doing under the desk, as employees walked in and out of his office. Never realizing what was going on. The times they had been caught, the employees were too embarrassed to repeat what they had seen. Their actions probably would have went on forever if it hadn't been for the unexpected visit of the owner.

Normally, she would have checked the door before they started their romp on the desk. But he seemed overly anxious to get started today and in the excitement she had forgotten to check. They had hardly begun when Edward heard a loud intake of air coming from the direction of the door. As he looked up he saw the stunned face of the owner of the company. Before he could even move the owner had fired him. Then in the next breath reconsidered and told him he was being transferred to the European office, unless he really did want to be fired. No one had wanted to take the position, he'd said. But now he had the perfect solution, Edward. "And you can take your trashy assistant with you", he continued. He nearly spit the word 'assistant' as he said it.

Upon hearing this, his assistant straightened up from her position on the desk and addressed him in her most "charming self". Asking if there was anything at all she could do to change his mind? Walking seductively towards him as she spoke. Gently stroking his arm as she stood within inches of him. Making sure he had understood her offer. He visibly flinched as she touched him. Then jerked his arm free of hers as he stormed out of the room. Replying, "I think you have done more than enough already".

Edward was furious with her. Not only had they been busted, but they had been exiled to Europe. Somewhere in the Middle East to be exact. Stupid Bitch! She didn't even have sense enough to lock the door before they started. He had the bad luck of picking some of the most stupid women in the world. First, his girlfriend killed the wrong people and then his secretary had sex on his desk without locking the door first!! He sure couldn't have hired her for her brains. And to top it off, she had tried to proposition the owner! He was sure he couldn't have picked two dumber women if he'd tried.

But now he was stuck with her. She was all he had left, and unfortunately he would probably end up being stuck with the girlfriend as well. He couldn't risk leaving her state side to tell all she knew. He would have to figure out a way to take her too. The thoughts of both of them in a foreign country with him, was almost too much to take. Sex with the two of them had been great! His plan had worked out perfectly. Not only had his girlfriend been eager to let his secretary join them, she had selfishly keep her to herself several times while he was forced to watch. They both loved the arrangement between them and enjoyed one another's company as much as his.

He couldn't say he was really disappointed though. Watching the two of them make love was a real turn on. He was so hot after watching them together, he could barely wait his turn. They seemed to enjoy watching him squirm and would draw out their love making together, for what seemed like hours. Just when he thought he couldn't wait another minute, they would motion for him to join them and together would take him to places he didn't know existed. That part of his life was a dream come true. But living with them 24/7 was another thing.

He didn't do well living with a wife or lovers day to day. He needed more space than that. He felt smothered being around women that long. Listening to their nagging and whining all the time drove him nuts. Too bad he couldn't just call them up when he needed sex and then ignore them the rest of the time. But common sense told him that would never work, so now he was stuck with them.

He knew there was no way Savannah would travel half way around the world with him. Not in the condition their marriage was in and certainly not when she found out why he had been transferred. He would just as soon not cross that bridge until he came to it! But even if that hadn't been the case, there was no way she would have raised their girls in a foreign country where they couldn't speak the language, even if some English was spoken there. She wouldn't put them through such a hardship. They had always been her first priority in life and she would do anything to protect them.

Then there was the matter of his cousin and nieces death. She still hadn't come to terms with it. She had really taken their deaths hard. They had been as close as her own family to her. A day didn't go by that she wasn't completely overcome by grief. Collapsing into uncontrollable weeping. It would be a long time before she recovered from their deaths.

He had been devastated too. But life goes on and he had tried to put it all behind him. He didn't want to go to Europe either, but until he could find another job, he was stuck there. He always seemed to land on his feet though and he was sure this time would be no different. After all he could have been fired, but he wasn't. That had to count for something. He had high hopes he would be back in the states before he knew it.

CHAPTER 16

Edward hadn't been given much time to get his affairs in order. In less than a week he and his secretary were on their way to the Middle East. The owner had a place he stayed in when he visited that office and had generously agreed to let Edward use it. Under the circumstances Edward was surprised by the owners generosity. But graciously accepted it.

He hadn't been able to tell Savannah the truth about the situation and had lied about it being a temporary situation that would last only as long as it took for him to get the European office in order. "A few months at most", he'd said. He lied so naturally it even sounded convincing to him.

His girlfriend had been the easiest to convince. She thought the whole thing was an exciting adventure and couldn't wait to leave. She now had him all to herself and couldn't imagine a more perfect situation. A dream come true for her. It wasn't like she had anything keeping her here. Or anything she was leaving behind. She lived in a dumpy apartment, working at a dead end job. Where ever she was going had to be better than this. She had a spring in her step as she and her companions boarded the plane. "Bring it on!

Let the adventure begin!" she thought with a smile. But her companions faces didn't seem to share her same excitement.

Edward in fact, felt like he had just been sentenced to "Life Without Parole". The Death Penalty looked good at this point. But he had to get a grip on himself and quit being so gloomy or he wasn't going to make it. This was the hand he had been dealt and he would just have to make the best of it.

His resolve nearly collapsed as his patience came severely close to snapping. The endless flight to his new home was becoming a test of endurance. He was hoping to kick back and relax a little before they landed, but it was not to be. His two companions would not shut-up. They talked like a blaring radio, turned up way too loud and slightly off channel. He tried to ignore them, but they were having none of it. He was going to be part of the conversation whether he liked it or not.

They had a million questions. Where exactly were they going? Where would they be staying? Were there any stores or shops nearby? How far did American money go there? Unlike a radio, he couldn't turn them off. So on they went with their endless questions. After a while it all seemed to blend into one. He could see their lips moving, but couldn't really make out what they were saying. He just nodded every once in a while to make them think he was still listening. Praying to God they would soon go hoarse and loose their voices. Giving him some peace at last.

When they finally landed, all he wanted to do was flee from them. Maybe he'd get lucky and lose them in the crowd! But no such luck. They stuck to him like glue. There was no escaping them. As he descended the plane he could immediately feel how hot the country was. It was hotter than any place he had ever been. It felt like a sauna and dust was blowing everywhere. He had gotten general directions to the office from the owner, but he had a feeling they weren't going to be much help. He felt like he was at the end of the world. Dropped off by a spaceship on Mars. He had realized it probably wouldn't be like home. But these conditions were truly barbaric and their clothes made them stick out like neon signs.

He couldn't believe he was actually going to have to live here. Had anyone at this office really volunteered to come here? He couldn't imagine it was possible. He knew he couldn't share these dreadful conditions with Savannah or the girls. It was too terrible to share with anyone. He'd send them a cheery little letter telling them how pleased he was to be here and what a great opportunity it was going to be for him. It was all fiction of course, but what else could he do? It would be some of the best creative writing he'd ever written.

They decided to stop by the apartment first to unload their luggage, before going to the office. His companions were still chattering as they walked behind him and he was going to lose his mind if they didn't shut-up soon. The stress of the place alone was bad enough, but add in their constant chatter and it made his head hurt so bad from listening to them, he thought it was going to explode. The sight of the apartment didn't improve his mood either. If he had known just how bad the apartment was going to be, he would have stepped right back on the plane and gone home. Job or no job!

The whole apartment was no bigger than his living room back home. The bathroom was so small that when you showered the whole room got wet. Toilet, sink and floor. There was a drain in the floor, but he would come to realize it rarely worked right. Leaving water standing on the floor for days. And forget about hot water. There was a heated water tank above the shower with an open pilot light flame going to it. It didn't really heat the water though, it just took the chill off of it. And if you stood up too straight in the shower, the flame would singe your hair.

There was only one bedroom, if you could call it that. It had a door for the bed, propped up on bricks which fit perfectly in the room. With no space on any side of the bed. You had to crawl in and out of the bed just to enter the room. They quickly decided this wasn't going to work and removed the door and bricks from the room. Using the room as a closet instead. Moving the bedroom to the living room. With no television or electronic equipment, there wasn't much to put in there anyway. The lighting in the apartment was open wires with light bulbs on the ends. The kitchen was just more of the same nightmare. He had seen horror movies that weren't this scary.

He couldn't believe this was his new home. Nothing could have prepared him for something this bad. How he was going to survive his stay over here, he had no idea. The owner must be having a good laugh knowing the Hell he had sent him to. The only bright spot of the whole afternoon was his companions stunned expressions. They were so shocked by what they saw, they were speechless. What a welcome sound that was!

The nightmare continued as they visited the office. His secretary tried to back out of going by saying she felt sick. But he just ignored her. She had gotten them into this mess, so she could just get use to this Hell-Hole! They were going to be here a while. He had to admit she didn't look too well. But he was in a really bad mood and figured she could just "suck it up" and get on with it. Just like he was trying to do.

They had left the girlfriend back at the apartment to put everything away. She wasn't anxious to get out in this heat either. So she volunteered to stay behind. Not that they had air-conditioning or anything. But at least she could stay out of the Sun and try to cool off. Walking in this weather felt like standing in a blast furnace and she refused to be a part of it. "I'll skip this one, thank you very much," she had said. She was sure he would drag her into the running of the office soon enough. No sense in rushing things.

By the time they had walked to the office his secretary looked ashen. They had stopped several times along the way, because she had become ill and thrown-up. He thought she just needed to toughen-up. Having no idea she was pregnant with his child. Believing with a little water and rest from the Sun she would be fine. He was sure of it.

They spent a while touring the office and meeting the employees. With her complaining the whole time. She was becoming a real "pain". Complaining about every step they took. Begging to set down every few steps and finally demanding to go back to the apartment. Insisting she was too sick to continue. He finally gave in. With all her whining she was really useless anyway. He had only continued to make her stay so she could feel some of the misery she had caused him. Now her constant complaining was taking away any satisfaction he could have felt from making her miserable too.

He stayed on for several more hours and then left

himself. It felt considerably hotter as he exited the building. Hotter than he remembered it being when they arrived. He hadn't gone far when he saw a crumpled body along the roadside. As he neared the body he was shocked to see it was his secretary. She was barely breathing and her body felt on fire. He took off the shirt he was wearing and draped it over her head to keep the Sun from baring down on her even more. Then ran back to the office for help.

They contacted the nearest Medical Center which arrived shortly and carted her off on a cot. Deciding she was too ill to wait for motorized transportation to arrive. They worked on her frantically when she arrived at the clinic, but it was pretty clear she wasn't going to make it. She was unconscious and had lost a lot of blood. A miscarriage brought on by a heat stroke, they thought. They did all they could for her, but she was too far gone by the time they had gotten her and died shortly after she arrived.

They were little more than a Third World hospital and didn't have the equipment to treat someone so seriously ill. It was sad losing someone that young, but they saw deaths like this every day. It was just a fact of life in this part of the world. People grieved in their own personal way and then moved on with their lives. They were too poor to have the luxury of grieving too long. If they did, the rest of their families may suffer the same fate.

Edward however, was in a state of shock when they broke the news to him. He was beside himself with grief and felt like a murderer. No better than his girlfriend. If he hadn't been so mad at her and self-absorbed with his own misery, he might have recognized just how sick she really was. But now she was dead and it was all his fault. He was sure he was going to Hell for killing her and all the other terrible things he had done.

Up until now he had thought there was still time to save himself. But this was too terrible a sin to be forgiven from and he had finally strayed too far to be saved from eternal damnation. He would be separated for eternity from his wife and daughters. Not that he had ever put a lot of time into them. But this was forever and now it was too late.

He didn't know how he was going to tell his girlfriend what had happened. But who was she to pass judgment anyway? She had already killed three people! He had a ways to go before he caught up to her. They were both bad to the bone and murderers going to Hell. But he couldn't worry about that now. He had to worry about how he was going to move on from here.

He knew he couldn't run the office without a secretary and she was all he had left. She would just have to pitch in and help out. Like it or not, there was nothing else that could be done. If he couldn't keep the office running they would both be out on the streets and it wouldn't take much more for the owner to let him go. He was already skating on thin ice. One more screw-up and he was sure it would be his last.

CHAPTER 17

His girlfriend was saddened by the news when he told her, but agreed something needed to be done fast. She readily agreed to help him, but she was terrible. She had never worked in an office or any place that even closely resembled one. Her only saving grace was her likeable personality. She made friends easy and most of the staff were more than willing to help her out. Edward had originally tried to show her the ropes himself, but soon realized it was an impossible task.

He had, had to make lists each day for her to follow, just so she would know how to start the day. But even with the written list, she had no idea how to complete the tasks. Edward became so frustrated with her lack of skills that he finally passed her training off to another employee. The employee seemed to make some progress with her, but she was not a fast learner. She caught on about as fast as a five year old would have. But the employees' patience never seemed to fade and Edward had hope that they just might make it. He made a note to himself to reward this employee with a big fat raise. If anyone deserved one, he sure did!

They struggled on with putting the office back together. The work was not being done with any sort of speed or even very well for that matter, but it was getting done and that was a step in the right direction. Hopefully the office would soon be up and running again and they could start concentrating on bigger issues.

The owner had already scheduled a trip for Edward and his secretary, having no idea that the real secretary was no longer there. Edward hadn't had the nerve to tell him what was really going on. He had hoped to stall for time so when the owner did find out, the office would be running smoothly enough that it wouldn't matter. He figured he had at least a few weeks before the truth came out because the owner was sending them to Beirut, Lebanon.

They were to meet with an Arab Sheik who would be staying at the American Hotel in Beirut. The same place Edward and his girlfriend would be staying. The Sheik was interested in buying drill bits for the numerous oil wells he had in the Middle East. If Edward could land this contract, it would mean a huge profit for the company. Edward was a great businessman, but with all his resent screw-ups he wasn't feeling as cocky as he normally would. He hoped he could pull this off without another disastrous ending.

They were actually both excited to be going to Beirut. They had heard some really good things about it. Including all the great night life it had and the bars and restaurants that were rumored to be some of the best in the world. It sounded like party time to Edward and he couldn't wait to get away from this place. He was going to extend his trip for as long as he could. Maybe he would get lucky and the Sheik would have more on his mind than just business too.

When Edward and his girlfriend, arrived in Beirut they couldn't have been happier. What a lovely city it was.

They meet the Arab Business Man at the Hotel as planned. Then spent the rest of the day touring with him and his personnel tour guide. They finished the night by hopping from nightclub to nightclub and sampling some of the best cuisine in the world.

It hadn't taken many drinks at the clubs that night before it became very clear that the Arab and his girlfriend were really enjoying one another. Maybe a little too much. Their actions were far too intimate for public display. As the nasty glares from the other club goers showed soon his girlfriend and her new friend excused themselves and went back to his room. Edward was only half interested in when or if they would return.

In truth he was in no hurry to get her back. He was relieved when they hadn't immediately returned. He desperately needed a break from her. The Arab was welcome to her for as long as he wanted. He just hoped the Arab would return long enough to place his order for the drill bits.

He needn't have worried though, because on the third day he received a note from the business man with a very generous order for the drills bits. Including payment. He explained where they were to be delivered and how soon he needed them. He also went on to say that he had grown very fond of Edward's girlfriend and had invited her to return home with him. Maybe only as an extended vacation or possibly more. They would be leaving immediately and hoped Edward understood the situation and it would not cause any problems between them. He had liked doing business with him and hoped they could continue doing business in the future. He also told Edward he was welcome to stay in the Hotel for the rest of the week. The room had already been paid for and it would be a shame for it to go unused and Edward to miss out on such a great opportunity. He again apologized for the short notice, but hoped the generous order would smooth things over between them. He wished him the best and hoped he enjoyed the rest of his stay.

Edward was sure that was the last time he would ever see his girlfriend. The Arab's place would have to be better than the "Hell Hole" they had been living in. It was also something she had always dreamed of having. A life of luxury with a man who really seemed to care about her. She must have been thrilled by the Arab's offer.

CHAPTER 18

She was indeed thrilled by the Arab's offer. Coming from a life of poverty and a daily struggle to survive, this was a dream come true for her. She would no longer be humiliated and degraded for being "Trailer Trash." A burdensome wasteful existence, echoed by the upper class. She could live like they did now and not continually be ridiculed for things she was powerless to change. She wasn't sure where they were going or what she would find when they got there, but it had to be better than the life she was living now. She had always been one to take chances and push the boundaries and it had served her well. No sense changing what had always worked. She had high hopes for this new adventure. When and if it came to an end, she was sure a new adventure would be right around the corner.

Edward should have gotten on a plane that day and left too. But he had no way of knowing what was about to happen. All he could think of was what a lucky break it had been for him to be rid of her. And as a bonus, he had been given an extended vacation in this beautiful city. But within hours his wonderful vacation would come to a tragic end. As Edward and his tour guide were walking around the city enjoying the sites, they began to hear cheering crowds and cars honking their horns. When the tour guide finally got one of the cars to stop, he asked what was going on.

Their answer caused all the color to drain from his face. He looked as thought he might pass out. When he returned, he told Edward what they had said. Several Israeli solders had been kidnapped by Lebonese soldiers and all Hell was about to break loose.

Edward thought the guide might just be over reacting. But the guide refused to be reasoned with and said he was going home. He needed to make sure his family was safe. He warned Edward that if he had any sense, he would leave immediately too.

Edward smiled and thanked him for the warning, but told him he was staying. He was sure everything would be just fine and he was having way too good a time to leave now. The guide shook his head in disbelief and fled with the rest of the crowd.

Edward was unconcerned with the Mayham and decided to continue his tour alone. But as the day wore on he could see that his tour guide was not the only one worried. People were closing up shops and businesses, leaving the city anyway they could. Not bothering to take anything but the clothes on their backs. By the time Edward realized what a serious situation it might really be, all the transportation in the city was already gone. He suddenly realized that his only hope of getting out of the city was to fly out on a private plane. But as he walked towards the airport and entered the gates, an incoming missile exploded on the runway.

Edward was dead in an instant. Never knowing what had hit him. His girlfriend and her new love were well away from the city by then and never knew Edward was among the dead that day.

CHAPTER 19

Savannah had just been given the news that Edward was dead. She had seen the bombing in Beirut, but never dreamed Edward would be there.

Edward's boss had stopped by to tell her the news, as soon as his office had received it. He explained how sorry he was about Edward's death and how sorry he was it had happened. As Savannah half said out loud to herself, "He should never have taken that transfer."

Edward's boss looked somewhat surprised. He asked if Edward had told her he volunteered for the transfer? She slowly shook her head yes. The boss dropped his head, as he gently took her hand and explained what had really happened. He wasn't about to let Savannah live out her life with the guilt that she should have stopped him.

When he finished telling her what really happened, she broke down in tears. Sobbing almost uncontrollable. It might seem to outsiders that she was truly in love with Edward. But the tears had nothing to do with love. She was so revolted by his final act of betrayal she could hardly hold it in. She had spent so many years cleaning up his messies, she should have realized he was capable of this. But this seemed to evil for even Edward.

The thought surprised her. After years of cleaning up his messies and dealing with the embarrassment and humiliation he caused, nothing he did should have been surprising. But this type of Evil, took evil to a whole new level. She couldn't believe how stupid and misguided she had been all these years, no matter how hard she tried. She just couldn't wrap her mind around someone who was just truly bad. Not one redeeming quality. The worst he acted the happier he seemed to be.

She had refused to believe all these years anyone would choose to be that bad. Even the "worst of the worst" must have some redeeming quality. But even as she thought this, she knew deep inside it wasn't true. She tried to deny this fact her whole life, but Edward's life spoke for itself. He was one train wreck after another and seemed to enjoy every bit of it.

What a wasted life she had spent. In spite of Edward, she had always been a wonderful and caring mother. But Edward's life of chaos had somehow taken over her life. She wasn't sure who she was anymore. She was so busy cleaning up their lives she had lost herself along the way.

Today's admission by Edward's boss had brought it all chasing down. There was no real Savannah left. Only a shadow of Edward's clean-up team. The realization made her feel sick inside. How could she have cared so much about how Edward's behavior would effect her family, that she lost track of who she was? Was she really that stupid and naive or had her chaotic life just knocked her off track? She wanted to believe that it was the best part of her that just wouldn't let her give up. Wouldn't let her fully realize just how bad things were.

It wasn't that she loved Edward. She had stopped loving him years ago. In fact the news of his death was actually a relief. She was finally free of him. He had never really been a part of their family anyway. He was more like a distant relative you seen now and then, but didn't really know that well.

She also knew deep inside, that part of her just couldn't admit what a terrible mistake she had made. What a terrible judge of character she had been. What a sad father she had provided for her children. She had thought at the time she was making a good choice, but she couldn't have been more wrong.

She had wasted most of her life and that of her children worrying about how Edward's bad behavior would make people think of them. But there was no more worrying now.

Any ounce of pride she had left, had been destroyed today. She had almost been overcome by it all. She had spent her married life being scared and afraid. And now all her worst fears had been realized.

It might take her some time to regroup, but she was determined to never be that scared and afraid again. To never allow this kind of Evil to touch her life again. She prayed God would give her the strength and wisdom to see it coming next time before it could touch her.

She had time left to right the wrong this life had dealt her. To have the life she once dreamed of. Not the life she had hoped for and miserably failed at. Would true love ever come her way and finish the dream she once had? Or would it always be a struggle between good and evil? A struggle she could never win. After all, she had lived her life trying to see only the good in people and ended up with Edward.

Did she really not know who he was? Was she really that bad at judging people? Or did she just want to believe that patience and goodness would always win over evil? Was it just easier and less frightening to believe this kind of evil didn't exist?

It was hard to believe even now that there were simply some people who didn't want to be good. They never did! And no amount of goodness and patience would win them over. They simply lure you in and drag you down their road of destruction, while you never realize what's happening.

You continue to pray and fret and beat yourself up for not being able to reach them and turn their lives around. Never realizing they already know what you are trying to do and they simply don't care. They know you have no idea who they really are and they will use that knowledge to their own advantage. Their evil looks so normal you never see it coming. It only seems fair that kind of evil should have a mark on it, so you would know it when you seen it.

But it doesn't work that way and you have to forgive yourself for being tricked and drawn in. Somehow evil can always smell out good. But we can't stop being good just because we won't always be able to protect ourselves. Otherwise we become just as bad as they are and we end up losing twice.

It is hard to see what we don't know. But we have to keep trying. We're the good guys in all this and the world needs more good guys. If we stop being good just to stay safe, everybody loses. My children deserve better than that and so do I.

I need to take the second chance God has given me and do it right this time. Not let myself get off course by all the busyness of life. I need to stay the course and keep my eyes on the path he has chosen for me. Knowing that whatever path he has chosen, will be better than anything I could have chosen for myself.

The End